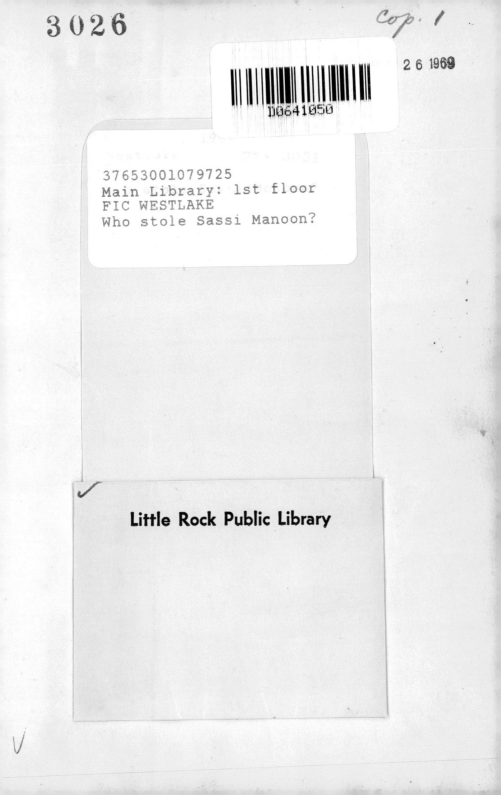

WHO STOLE SASSI MANOON?

By the same author

THE MERCENARIES

KILLING TIME

361

KILLY

PITY HIM AFTERWARDS

THE FUGITIVE PIGEON

THE BUSY BODY

THE SPY IN THE OINTMENT

GOD SAVE THE MARK

THE CURIOUS FACTS
PRECEDING MY EXECUTION
AND OTHER FICTIONS

Who Stole

SASSI
MANOON?

by Donald E. Westlake

RANDOM HOUSE / NEW YORK

This (like me) is for Sandy

No picture shall be produced which will lower the moral standards of those who see it. Hence the sympathy of the audience should never be thrown to the side of crime, wrongdoing, evil or sin. Correct standards of life shall be presented on the screen, subject only to necessary dramatic contrasts. Law, natural or human, should not be ridiculed, nor shall sympathy be created for its violation.

> *A Code to Govern the Making of Motion and Talking Pictures by The Motion Picture Producers of America, Inc.*
> March 31, 1930

Stolen sweets are best.

> Colley Cibber: *The Rival Fools*
> 1709

Contents

PART TWO—People

Schedule

MONTEGO BAY FILM FESTIVAL

Saturday, December 2nd, 8:00 P.M.; black tie dinner presented by the Festival Committee for the judges and most important guests—speeches—presentation of members of the jury

> 11:00 P.M.; showing in the Main Hall of *The Sun Never Sets,* official British entry

Sunday, December 3rd, 3:00 P.M.; *Tin Cup and River,* official Indian entry
6:00 P.M.; *Blondie Brings Up Baby,* 1939, retrospective
9:00 P.M.; *The Old Lions,* official West Germany entry

Monday, December 4th, 3:00 P.M.; *Miasma,* official
Italian entry
6:00 P.M.; *Blondie Meets the
Boss,* 1939, retrospective
9:00 P.M.; *Giggle,* invited
British entry

Tuesday, December 5th, 3:00 P.M.; *The Beautiful
Sewer,* official Polish entry
6:00 P.M.; *Blondie Takes a
Vacation,* 1939, retrospective
9:00 P.M.; *Tomorrow the
World,* official Egyptian entry

Wednesday, December 6th, 3:00 P.M.; *Murder Times
Murder,* official French entry
6:00 P.M.; *Blondie Has Servant
Trouble,* 1940, retrospective
9:00 P.M.; *The Crippled
Samurai,* official Japanese entry

Thursday, December 7th, 3:00 P.M.; *Slime and Scorpion,*
invited American entry
6:00 P.M.; *Blondie on a Budget,*
1940, retrospective
9:00 P.M.; *Naked Afternoons,*
official Swedish entry

Friday, December 8th, 3:00 P.M.; *The Boots of the
Elk,* official Russian entry

x

6:00 P.M.; *Blondie Plays Cupid*,
1940, retrospective
9:00 P.M.; *Revolution!*, official
Mexican entry

Saturday, December 9th, 3:00 P.M.; *Kangaroo Court*,
official Australian entry
6:00 P.M.; *Blondie Goes Latin*,
1941, retrospective
9:00 P.M.; *Abortion, Italian
Style*, invited Italian entry

Sunday, December 10th, 3:00 P.M.; *Alive and Well*,
official Argentine entry
6:00 P.M.; *Blondie in Society*,
1941, retrospective
9:00 P.M.; *Nuns and Harlots*,
invited French entry

Monday, December 11th, 8:00 P.M.; award dinner
11:00 P.M.; *The Big Knife*,
1955, retrospective

JURY

Sir Walter Ridley, President, Great Britain—Chairman of
the Board, British Gong Films—Diffuse Television
Enterprises—Magnacar Wicker Furniture Ltd.

Claude-Ferrie Massagu, France—Editor, *Oeuvres de
Cinema*

G. Chinovvikov, Union of Soviet Socialist Republics—
Director of Film Secretariat, Murmansk

Ernst Klarg, West Germany—Film Curator, University
Museum, University of Kaiserläutern

Mobara Tarachapu, India—film director (*Passivity*, 1966;
Mournful Pan, 1967)

Theramin Kilpatrick, Australia—Chairman, Film Censor-
ship Board, Brisbane

Sassi Manoon, United States of America—actress (*Meet the
Gobs*, 1960; *Bubbletop*, 1962; *All These Forgotten*,
1964; *Caper*, 1966)

PART ONE

MACHINES

(1)

S.T.A.R.N.A.P.

There was no one aboard the *Nothing Ventured IV* when Kelly came striding down the dock toward it in the sunshine. A gleaming white forty-foot Nelson & Almen cabin cruiser built in 1940, the ship had been modernized somewhere along the line and now boasted twin GM 6-71 diesels, air conditioning and a fully equipped cockpit. Kelly had owned it seven months now, and in that time no one had ever stepped aboard it other than himself. It had been his hideaway, his true home, his secret world. Today all that was about to change, and in his heart Kelly didn't like it.

That was part of the reason he'd come here so early, almost an hour before the one o'clock scheduled for the meeting. He wanted to be alone in this place just a little longer, before other people intruded into his ship and his life, before his plans stopped being harmless dreams and began to move into reality, where there was no turning back.

Kelly, a slender studious spectacled young man wearing gray sneakers, khaki slacks, a white polo shirt, and clip-on sunglasses, stepped carefully from dock to deck and paused to look around, but so far as he could tell he was unobserved. The Florida sun beat down as though to deny that the calendar could read November, and amid the sparkle and gleam of all the boats at this marina south of Miami Beach the *Nothing Ventured IV* shone in silver and white anonymity, looking no different from any other craft moored here. But it was different, in ways that only Kelly knew.

Kelly ducked his head and trotted down the steep steps into the main cabin, a clean well-lighted place with green carpeting and maple woodwork. It was hot down here, so he switched on the air conditioner before removing his clip-ons and going to the small and crowded forward cabin, the center of his secret life. He turned on the hanging light and smiled at the machine.

"Hello, Starnap," he said.

He sat at the console, his fingers resting gently on the keys. The machine was silent, but he could hear water lapping at the sides of the boat, he could feel the gentle motion of the ship tugging at its ropes. It soothed him to be here. "Well," he said to the machine, "today's the big day." He shook his head with a rueful smile. "I certainly hope you're right," he said.

Kelly, Kelly Bram Nicholas IV, son of Kelly Bram Nicholas III, grandson of Kelly Bram Nicholas II, great-grandson of Kelly Bram Nicholas, hated everybody but loved machines. Given a father bowed under by the weight of being the third Kelly Bram Nicholas in a row, and a domineering mother whom only a psychiatrist could love, the present Kelly Bram Nicholas—jeeringly called Ivy at school because of the IV at the end of his name—grew up with the knowledge that machines could be trusted but people never. Where is there a human being with a ring in his neck that when you pull it he says, "I love you"? No-where. But there's a Casper the Friendly Ghost doll that does just exactly that. And with feeling. And why? Because within its lifelike plastic exterior there exists a tiny brilliant machine.

Kelly was himself in many ways a tiny brilliant machine, and if all his scientific, electronic, mechanical, and chemi-cal endeavors seemed to end in destruction it did not neces-sarily mean that all were failures. For though Kelly didn't particularly want to destroy machines—he liked machines —and though he didn't particularly want to destroy human beings—that was something other people did—it is undeni-ably true that Kelly did want to destroy *something*. He himself wasn't sure what.

Life for Kelly so far had been an endless series of Pyrrhic victories. His home life had been marred by the fact that he and his mother had what might be called a personality conflict, making him perhaps the only only child in modern America who was *not* spoiled, and his schooling had been blighted by his having been one of those unathletic know-it-alls who are too smart for their own good. Teachers don't like to be outstripped by their pupils, and children don't like children who know too much. Given also a vague and ineffectual father who didn't want to hear about anybody else's problems and who preferred not be home very much anyway, it was perhaps inevitable that Kelly should grow up bitter, lonely, brilliant, and acidly anti-social.

After being thrown out of his fourth engineering college for learning not wisely but too well, Kelly had found himself at his mother's instigation cut off from further access to the family funds. Further schooling, already unnecessary, was now made impossible. Unfortunately, the sort of explosive blue-sky research that had been occasionally available in college labs was now also impossible. How was he to continue his experiments? How was he to support himself? Work was out of the question, since his education had left him unequipped for gainful labor and he was, besides, socially unadapted to deal with his fellow man.

It was then he'd decided there was no possible future for him but a life of crime (short) to be followed by a life of ease (long). And for his first partner in crime what possible choice could he have made but the one he did? A machine. In fact, Starnap.

Starnap had been built by Kelly, alone, within this boat, which he'd bought fourth-hand—but still overpriced—in Atlantic City. The ship had taken money, and so had Starnap, and the money had come from a variety of sources. Blackmail, for one, upon the adulterous person of his father, who had sighed and paid and said not a word. His automobile, a creature Kelly had loved and slaved over, went on the block, and so did his hi-fi set. Reluctantly but grimly he had sold all of what might have been the finest and most complete collection of horror and science-fiction comic books in the world. And finally, during his college days, he had patented two small inventions—a kind of self-sealing milk carton and a pesticide sprayer—both of which brought in small annual amounts, and these now he also sold, too cheap.

Kelly had planned—and Starnap, when finished, had agreed with him—to commit only one crime, but that one large enough to keep him comfortably fixed the rest of his life. What the crime would be he didn't at first know, but he was sure he and his machine would find something worthy of their combined talents.

Once Starnap had been put together, therefore, Kelly began by feeding it *The New York Times,* both daily and Sunday, by the bale, by the truckload, till its memory banks were full to bursting with information on international affairs and sales at Ohrbach's and all the news that's fit to print. Only then, when Kelly considered the machine his intellectual equal, did they begin to consider the crime for which Starnap—not at that point yet named—had been brought into existence, and they studied the problem together for several weeks before at last making their decision.

Once the caper was chosen, however, a great disagreement occurred between them, one which almost caused a rift in their relations. Kelly, naturally, had wanted to pull the job himself, but Starnap had insisted upon assistants, two of them. Kelly had angrily demurred, but at last Starnap, with logic and patience, had brought him around and they had started their quest for a mob.

It had been Starnap's decision to limit themselves to people Kelly already knew, and in retrospect Kelly could see that that had been an intuitively brilliant move, as well as an indication that Kelly's own tendency toward paranoia had been transferred to his machine. The problem was one of trust, for it seemed to both Starnap and Kelly that a professional criminal might not consider himself honor-bound to deal fairly with someone who by lack of experience could be considered an amateur and therefore an outsider. Better to compose the gang entirely of amateurs, and of individuals already known and proven trustworthy under other circumstances.

Into Starnap, then, Kelly had fed every scrap of information he could find or remember about everybody he'd ever known at all well. There weren't that many, given Kelly's personality, but from the data presented it Starnap had at last produced two names. These two, Starnap had reported, not only had special qualifications and talents which would make them valuable members of the team, but also their personalities and histories were such that they were very likely to fall in with the sort of scheme Kelly had in mind.

Kelly had been out of touch with both prospects for some time, but they hadn't been hard to track down, and he had been heartened to see that neither seemed to be doing very well for himself. Following Starnap's plan for making contact he had sent letters to them both, containing a plane ticket and a twenty-dollar bill. The letters, which weren't signed, had stated merely that there might be profit if the recipient were to come to a meeting at such and such a place at such and such a time, airline ticket and expense money enclosed. The implication was of something shady, which meant that if either or both did show up they were probably already half-committed to an illegal consequence.

And now was the day. If they were coming, they would

be here at one o'clock. Kelly, sitting in reverie before Star-nap, found himself wishing the planning stage could go on and on, that the actual recruiting of personnel, performing of the crime, could be forestalled indefinitely. The fun part, he was beginning to realize, was over.

A voice remarkably like that of Charles Laughton abruptly broke into his thoughts, calling from up on deck, "Mis-tah *Chris*-tian!"

"That's Frank," Kelly told Starnap, getting to his feet and looking at his watch. Five minutes to one. He'd been mooning down here almost an hour.

With a last look at Starnap, wishing he'd built a voice box into the machine so it could have taken over this interview itself now, Kelly switched off the light and went out to the main cabin, shutting the door behind him. He went over to the stairs and called, "Down here."

The young man who came trotting down the steps was Kelly's age and height, but there the similarity ended. Frank was blond, open-faced, cheerful and somewhat stocky of build. He was wearing brown loafers, tan slacks, a short-sleeved white shirt open at the throat, and wraparound sunglasses with white rims. He removed these glasses when he reached the foot of the stairs and said, "Kelly! You're the one?"

"I'm the one," Kelly said. Nervousness made him short of words.

Frank stuck his hand out, saying, "It's been a while, Kelly. The last time I heard from you was when you wanted to sell the comics. You get rid of them?"

"Yes. Eventually."

"I would have liked to help you out," Frank said, "but

(9)

DONALD E. WESTLAKE

I've been out of that business for a long while now." He
no longer sounded at all like Charles Laughton.

"I know."

Frank looked around the cabin. "This your boat? It looks
good."

"Yes."

Frank turned back to Kelly. "So what is it?" he said.

Kelly wasn't ready. Stammering a little, he said, "What's
what?"

"The letter," Frank said. "The ticket. The twenty dollars.
It isn't to sell me comic books."

"No. Uh—"

"*Anyone here?*"

It was another voice from up on deck, and Kelly leaped
gratefully at the interruption, shouting, "Yes! We're down
here."

Frank, watching the steps with some curiosity, said,
"Another one?"

"I don't think you know him," Kelly said, and the third
man joined them. "Robby," said Kelly. "Nice to see you
again."

Robby stopped three steps from the bottom. "Kelly," he
said. "Well, I'll be damned."

Robby could have been Harry Belafonte's younger
brother, brown and lithe and handsome, but with a somewhat more sour smile. He was wearing black oxfords, dark
gray trousers with a knifelike crease, white shirt, narrow
silver tie, light blue sport jacket, and wire-framed sunglasses with blue lenses. He was carrying a small blue bag
that said *Lufthansa* on the side.

Kelly pointed to the bag. "You've never been overseas,"
he said.

(10)

"Swiped it at the airport," Robby said. He came down the last three steps, dropped the bag, removed his sunglasses, shook Kelly's hand, and turned expectantly toward Frank. He moved gracefully, with social calm, the kind of young man whose major at college was women.

Kelly made the introductions: "Frank Ashford, Robby Creswel. I knew Frank when he used to be a used-magazine dealer, when we were both in our teens. Robby and I were at Sherman Tech together for a semester."

"Till you blew up the dormitory," Robby said. "Why all the secrecy, with the letter and all? Why not just call me on the telephone?"

"Just the question I was asking when you got here," Frank said.

Kelly had rehearsed this part, he and Starnap had decided the best method of approach. "Let me tell you in a way that might sound roundabout," he said.

"Oh, boy," said Frank. "You got anything to drink?"

"You'll find a well-stocked liquor cabinet there," Kelly told him. "I'll take a gin and tonic."

"Good. Robby?"

"That sounds fine," Robby said.

Kelly watched them. Neither seemed more than idly curious. Would it work? He cleared his throat and said, "One reason we three are together here right now is that we have so much in common."

Frank looked up from the open refrigerator. "We do?"

Robby laughed and said, "You wouldn't know it to look at us."

"We all need money," Kelly said.

The other two lost their good humor. Frank shut the refrigerator door, not having gotten any ice, and said,

"What's that supposed to mean?"

"What it says."

Robby said, "What makes you think you know about me?"

"I know about you," Kelly told him. "I know about both of you. I won't start talking about you in front of each other, but I do know that neither of you has much money, neither of you has a good job or good prospects, and if you *did* have a chance at a good job you probably wouldn't want it. Frank, won't you make the drinks?"

Frank, suddenly sounding exactly like W. C. Fields, said, "Maybe I better. I have a feeling I'm going to need a drink soon." He opened the refrigerator door again, got the ice cubes out.

"You both want," Kelly said, "what I want. A lot of money. Enough money so we can retire and live on the interest and devote our lives to our private concerns without having to worry about jobs or rent or payments on this and that or any of the other money things that hold us down."

"Amen," said Robby.

Frank, opening the tonic bottles, said, "An annuity, that's what I want. I'm not greedy. Just enough to live on, that's all. I don't want yachts." He gestured at the cabin around them. "None of this stuff. I could live on ten thousand a year."

"Figuring a five percent return on investments," Kelly said, "conservatively, that is, you'd need a principal of two hundred thousand to earn ten thousand a year."

"That's a lot of dollars," Frank said. He poured gin over ice, tonic over gin.

Robby, a little smile playing around the corners of his mouth, 2said, *"You aren't leading up to something crooked, are you?"*

"Of course I am," Kelly said. *"Nobody can get two hundred thousand dollars legally."*

Frank brought the drinks, then raised his glass. *"To crime,"* he said, and his voice was suddenly that of Edward G. Robinson.

They drank.

Robby said, *"What sort of crime, Kelly?"*

"You'll have to tell me yes or no first," Kelly said. *"I can't tell you the details and then have you say no and go away."*

Frank said, *"Kelly, be realistic. I don't know about Robby, but I can't say yes or no till I hear it. I say yes, you say go shoot your old man."*

"Nobody will be killed," Kelly said. "Nobody will be injured." He pointed to the closed door to the front cabin. "In there," he said, "I have a computer, a small self-sufficient computer named Starnap. That stands for Selective Timed Abstract Reactional Neutronic Abduction Positioner."

"What's *that* stand for?" Frank said.

"I'll tell you in a minute," Kelly said. "The point is, that computer is going to plot the crime for us. A scientific crime. Starnap can consider every possible detail, every circumstance, every available possibility. It would take a hundred professional criminals a year to come up with a plan that Starnap could do, once we've put in all the information, in five minutes."

"Well, you haven't changed," Robby said. "You're still a mad scientist."

"Starnap works," Kelly said.

"I don't doubt it," Robby told him.

Frank said, "Just a second. As I understand it, you want to start a life of crime here, and—"

"One crime," Kelly told him. "One crime, big enough to give the three of us enough money to live on comfortably the rest of our lives."

"How much is that?" Robby said.

"Not quite two hundred eight-five thousand dollars each," Kelly said.

There was a little silence, 8and then Robby said, "Fort Knox?"

"Better than Fort Knox," Kelly told him. "Safer."

Frank said, "And nobody gets killed. Nobody gets hurt. And you've got a computer to do the planning."

"Yes."

"And we say either yes or no before you tell us what it is."

"Yes. And one more thing, we would have to leave here today. We'll have to be in the Caribbean tomorrow to start getting things organized. So you'll have to decide right now."

Robby said, "And if it's yes, we leave right away?"

"Yes."

Frank and Robby looked at one another.

Kelly said. "You'll probably want to think about it, maybe discuss it with each other. I'll go in here for a while; just knock if you want to talk to me."

"Sure," said Frank faintly. He seemed distracted.

Kelly went into the forward cabin and sat down at Starnap's console. "I think they'll go for it," he told the machine. He sipped at his gin and tonic. It was delicious.

Three minutes went by before the knock came at the door. Kelly got to his feet and opened the door, saying, "Want to see Starnap?"

Robby and Frank were both in the doorway. They gazed in at Starnap.

Kelly said, "It's my own design, really. An adaptation of components from IBM, Burroughs, Control Data, ITT, RCA, and National Cash Register."

"It looks like it knows a lot," Frank said. "It has that sort of look, you know what I mean?"

Kelly said, "Did you make up your minds?"

"We're in," Frank said, and Robby nodded.

"Good," Kelly said. "Let's go sit down out here."

They went out to the main cabin and sat down and Frank said, "Don't build up the suspense, Kelly. We said yes. What's the caper?"

Kelly said, "Do both of you know of a movie actress named Sassi Manoon?"

Robby laughed, and Frank said, "Know of her? For God's sake, she's like top box office of the entire world! Come out of your ivory tower, Kelly!"

"I'm not in an ivory tower," Kelly said. "I know how popular Sassi Manoon is. I wasn't sure you two did."

"We do," Robby said. "What's the pitch?"

"We're going to steal her," Kelly said.

(2)

Windows

From her hotel-room picture window Sassi Manoon could see Las Vegas, which was too bad, because she didn't like Las Vegas and didn't want to be in Las Vegas. She preferred to look the other way, at her luggage all packed and ready to go. If only she could remember where she was going.

Sassi Manoon, thirty-two years old, beautiful, rich, well tended, famous and beloved of millions, hated to admit it but she was bored. She didn't want to be a cliché, and she knew the bored rich bitch was the most banal of clichés, but she couldn't help it. She was between movies, between husbands, and between destinations. All dressed up and too many places to go, none of them worth the trouble.

A few years back, when someone had asked Sassi if she'd ever thought of writing her biography, she'd answered, "Are you kidding? My biography came out of a Xerox machine." And in many ways it was true—her life seemed determinedly stock, the inevitable movie-star history. An orphan, she'd been brought up by foster parents on a North Dakota farm, and it was through winning a local beauty contest at fifteen that she'd been started on her way to fame and fortune. Along the way she'd had a teen-age marriage with a sailor met in San Diego, the marriage annulled after four months by mutual agreement, and followed in the sixteen years since by four other husbands, all of them now ex. She'd had small parts in three B movies and a dozen rotten television shows before her appearance as a poignant prostitute in *The Stark and the Wicked* had catapulted her to notoriety. The notoriety had gotten her Max Manning, one of the most brilliant agents in Hollywood, and Max Manning had gotten her stardom. Her price was now eight hundred fifty thousand dollars a film, and she made an average of one and a half films a year. She had stopped collecting magazines with her picture on the cover when the collection filled a small closet, and the last time she could remember having been excited about anything was four years ago when for a period of ten days she had seriously contemplated throwing the whole thing over and becoming a nun.

That was the problem, in a nutshell. Nothing *new* ever happened, there were no more mountains to climb, no more surprises around the corner. There weren't even any more corners, nothing but the straight flat road of assured success and guaranteed wealth and adulation. Working on a movie was still fun sometimes, depending on the script and the director and the other people in the cast, but the times in between were increasingly a drag.

"Maybe it's time to get married again," she told herself

(17)

now, and grimaced at the thought. A husband might be fun for a while, but sooner or later they became a cumbersome part of the luggage, a sort of Valpack with legs.

She laughed at that thought and went over to the window again, but it was still Las Vegas outside. She thought maybe she'd leave her money to teleportation research. Wouldn't it be nice to teleport? Switch instantly from where you are to where you want to be. No planes, no taxis, no bellboys, no interminable copies of the *Saturday Evening Post.*

Where would she like to be right now? Instead of Las Vegas, what place would she like to be looking at outside this window?

Well. Somewhere.

She'd come in from somewhere just yesterday. New York. In from New York on a plane with Benny Bernard and the Afghans. Benny had taught her gin, just as though nine other men hadn't taught her gin at various times in her life. He hadn't made a pass yet, but he would. Another inevitability.

Las Vegas. Sassi sighed, looking out the window. She was here because dear old Max had a new boy, and the boy had opened in a show here, and all Max's most prominent clients had dropped in for the premiere to assure the boy some decent press coverage. Sassi had had too much to drink, and right now for the life of her she couldn't remember what Max's new boy did. Sing? Dance? Tell jokes? Shadow box?

There was a knock at the door.

"Come in, Benny," Sassi called, daring fate to prove her wrong, and the door opened and Benny Bernard came in, saying, "We got an hour and a half to catch our plane."

Benny Bernard was second-generation movie, somebody's

nephew. When you don't know what to do with a useless relative, and he never finished high school, you get him into one of the craft unions, stagehand or sound technician or something like that. When you don't know what to do with a useless relative, and he's got a college diploma, you put him in public relations. Benny Bernard, somebody's nephew, had graduated four years ago from Cornell. For the last three months he'd been Sassi's traveling companion, her spokesman to the press.

"An hour and a half," Sassi said, turning away from the window. "I can't wait. Where do we go this time?"

"Jamaica," Benny said, surprised. "For Christ's sake, lovey, you were the one bitched to get this gig."

"Oh! The festival!"

"Of course the festival," Benny said. "You're a judge, your honor." He sat down in the white and gold Italian Provincial armchair near the window, and crossed his legs. His shoes buckled on the side, his tie was narrow enough to cut Levy's Jewish Rye, and he smelled of an aftershave with an Oriental name. Sunlight streamed in on him from the Las Vegas sky, but on Benny sunlight looked like radiation sickness.

"Judge," Sassi said, and smiled.

She'd forgotten all about it. Three months ago the letter had come from the Montego Bay Film Festival in Jamaica, asking her if she would be one of the judges this year, and she'd snapped at it. Something different, something new. Foreign movies, foreign movie people, another kind of movie world from the one she knew. And with some class attached to it, some intellectual cachet. Sassi had felt very honored, and when Max and the studio and everybody else

(19)

had tried to talk her out of it, claiming it wasn't for her and she should leave her time free for more important possibilities, she had refused to be dissuaded. She was going to be a judge, by God, at an important film festival.

"I don't know what you want with it," Benny was saying now. "Frankly, you don't need that kind of publicity. You're too big for stunts."

"I don't suppose you ever heard of the word prestige."

"I've heard of it," Benny said, "and I'll tell you what it is. Schweppervescence. But you ain't Commander Whitehead."

"You'd rather I took a year off and went to Actors' Studio?"

"As what? A prop?"

Sassi's face turned to stone. "I'll see you at the airport, Benny," she said.

Benny heard the ice in her voice, and he knew he'd gone that little bit too far. "It's a joke, lovey," he said, not quite hiding his nervousness. "Gay badinage, you know?"

"Pick up Kama and Sutra at the kennel. Send somebody up for my bags. Good-bye, Benny."

"Lady Godiva, don't get on that high horse. I'm sorry if I—"

Sassi picked up the phone and said, "Los Angeles, please. J-K Films."

"Sassi—"

She turned her back on him.

"All right," he said. "I'm going, I'm going. Our plane leaves at three, I've got the tickets."

When the door closed, she hung up. "What does *he* know?" she asked.

(3)

Fishing

"Ready?" asked Major ffork-Linton.

"Quite," said Miss Adelaide Rushby. She dibbled at her throat lace.

Outside, Jamaica lay obedient, a quiescent flying island in a crayola-blue sea. The yachts and clippers and runabouts were moored in rows, as though in the parking lot of a nautical supermarket. Inside, in the saloon of Major Alfred ffork-Linton's yacht *Redoubtable,* a cool dim British calm prevailed. A Victorian setting and a tweedy couple, Adelaide Rushby with her throat lace and her several chins, the Major with his leather elbow patches and peper-and-salt mustache.

"We're off, then," said the Major, and there was a knock at the door.

DONALD E. WESTLAKE

» The Major and Adelaide looked at one another. "It can't be anything," she whispered.

"Of course not," agreed the Major. "Foolish of us." He raised his voice and called, "Come in!"

The young man who diffidently entered was that nice Mr. Bullworth Spence from United Kingdom Films. He was casually dressed—short-sleeved white shirt, no tie—but at least he carried his pipe. "Afternoon, Major," he said. "Afternoon, Miss Rushby."

"Dear boy," the Major said, and Adelaide smiled a greeting.

"Are you off somewhere?" Spence asked. He was looking at the purse Miss Rushby was holding in her hands.

"Just a walk," she said.

"Well, I can't stay in any event," Spence said. "I just dropped round to tell you I did manage to wangle those tickets for that Italian film after all. *Abortion, Italian Style.*"

"Did you!" cried the Major. "Well done!"

"Also," said Spence, "to tell you there's a party at Sir Albert's tonight. In honor of Miss Sassi Manoon."

The Major and Adelaide looked at one another. She said to Spence, "But Miss Manoon is American."

"We want her for a co-production. American brawn, British brains. Besides, she's one of the festival judges. Would you be interested in coming?"

"To the party? We'd be delighted. Wouldn't we, Alfred?"

"Definitely," said the Major.

"Then what say I send a car round for you nineish."

"That would be lovely," said Adelaide. "And we do thank you."

(22)

"Not at all." He glanced at his watch. "Now I must be off," he said. "Picking her up at the airport, you know. See you this evening."

"This evening," the Major agreed.

Spence left, and Adelaide said, "Now, *that's* an unexpected blessing."

"Should prove helpful," the Major said. "Shall we see about our new neighbors?"

"Oh, yes! I'd forgotten."

They left *Redoubtable* and walked along the dock to the boat next door, a cabin cruiser named *Nothing Ventured IV* which had just arrived this morning with a crew of three, two whites and a black. The Major and Miss Rushby wanted to know if these new arrivals were likely to cause any trouble or hitch in the plan. They had previously paid calls on the other ships resident near their own, finding all of their passengers apparently harmless, and now it was time to reassure themselves about this latest addition.

All three young men were on deck on their vessel. The Major stopped at the foot of their gangplank and gazed at them. "ffork-Linton," he announced, smiling falsely. "And this is Miss Rushby."

"D'je do," said Adelaide, touching her throat lace.

There followed a long moment of awkward silence. The three young men appeared to be barbarians, total and entire. Not a one of them thought to introduce himself or respond in any way at all. In fact, they merely stood looking at one another, blank expressions on their faces, as the silence stretched into discomfort.

Dammit, it wasn't good manners to come aboard a man's vessel uninvited. The Major stood at the foot of the gangplank, waiting in vain for an invitation, and at last forced the issue by saying, "Neighborly visit, you know. Thought we'd drop in and say how d'je do to our new neighbors. We're from *Redoubtable* over there."

The black seemed suddenly to come awake, as though he'd been in a trance—did they take opiates?—and said, "Of course. Forgive us, Mr. ffork-Linton. Won't you and Miss Rushby come aboard?"

The white with the eyeglasses gave the black a swift and murderous look, which the Major chose not to see. Starting up the gangplank, Adelaide behind him, he said, "It's Major, actually."

"How do you do, Major?" The black extended a beige-palmed chocolate hand, saying, "Robert Creswel. And may I introduce Frank Ashford and Kelly Bram Nicholas IV."

"D'je do."

"How are you?"

"Plan to be in Jamaica long?" the Major asked. It was a bit disconcerting to have the Negro be the only one of the three to show any of the social graces, but the Major was not one to allow such irrelevancies to distract him from his main purpose.

"We're just here for the festival," said what-was-his-name? Ashford. Frank Ashford.

"Are you connected with the film world?"

"No," said the third, the one outlandishly called Kelly Bram Nicholas IV, while at the same time Frank Ashford was saying, "In a manner of speaking," and chuckling to himself as though he'd just remembered a joke. The IV character gave him a murderous look.

The black, Robert Creswel, said, "We're fans, is all."

Adelaide, her arm looped through the Major's, said,

"Have you any favorites among the film stars?"

This time, as IV was saying, "No," Frank Ashford was saying, "Sassi Manoon." More daggers were looked at him, and Robert Creswel hastily said, "I think my favorite is Sidney Poitier."

How those people stuck together. Worse than Jews. But odd that Ashford should mention Sassi Manoon, odd and troubling. Still, she was the biggest attraction at this festival, so perhaps it wasn't that odd after all.

Adelaide was saying, "We have so much admired your boat. So trim-looking."

It was an obvious, almost blunt, hint, and of course it was Creswel again who took it up. "Would you care for a look around?" he asked, and got one of IV's looks for his trouble. What was the matter with that one?

In any case, "We'd love to," said Adelaide, and the Creswel boy proceeded to take them on the grand tour. Frank Ashford, who appeared to be the comedian of the group, or at least to think of himself as the comedian of the group, made smallish nautical jokes as they moved along, and Kelly Bram Nicholas IV trailed after everybody, lowering and glowering.

The boat was not at all bad. The galley was small but well constructed, complete with electric refrigerator, and the main cabin was very nearly as comfortable as that on *Redoubtable*.

Only one oddity. The forward cabin was almost entirely given over to some sort of electronic machine, which looked vaguely menacing and science-fictionish in the swaying electric light. "Our fish finder," the Creswel boy said, showing it to them.

"Fish finder?" The Major stared at the machine in some

bewilderment. There seemed to be a great deal of it.

"Uses radar," Creswel said.

Ashford said, "You can really catch them with that."

"Interesting," said the Major, who found it boring. He never had liked to fish and couldn't understand those who did.

Back in the main cabin, it was Creswel who thought to offer drinks, which the Major refused with thanks. Then Ashford said, "You've been here long, Major?"

Ho ho, young man, now you're going to start pumping me. Well, no matter. "Just a few days," the Major said. "Like yourselves, we came here for the festival."

"And are *you* connected with the film world?"

"I have one or two friends in that business, but I myself am retired."

No one asked the Major what he was retired *from*. No one ever did.

They stayed a few minutes longer, chatting about this and that, but the Major was sure by now there was nothing to learn here nor any cause for alarm. Just three rich and idle young men gadding without purpose around the Caribbean in a boat undoubtedly purchased for one of them by a doting parent. The glares and glowers of Nicholas IV probably indicated that he was the boat's owner and was afflicted by the anti-social personality so frequently found in the offspring of the wealthy.

After a decent interval of conversation the Major and Adelaide made their departure. Back on their own boat, the Major said, "Well, they may be boors, but at least they're harmless."

"I rather liked them," said Adelaide.

"My dear," said the Major, "you like everybody. You'll probably even like Sassi Manoon."

*

"Fish finder!" Kelly said savagely, and pounded his fist on a handy countertop. The awful flatulent Englishman had finally toddled off, towing his tug Adelaide behind him, and Kelly at last could release the pent-up violence he'd been holding in check. "Fish finder!" he yelled. "You called Starnap a fish finder!"

"What did you want me to call it?" Robby asked him. "A Selective Timed Abstract Reactional Neutronic Abduction Positioner?"

"I didn't want you to call it anything. I didn't want those people on this boat at all. And then you go and *show* them Starnap!"

Robby, calm in the face of Kelly's storm, said, "It was the only thing we could do, Kelly. I'm sorry, but we were in a bind."

"Robby's right," Frank said, adding fuel to the fire.

"What's he so goddam right about?" Kelly demanded, not wanting to see their side of it. "Why'd we have to have them aboard at all? Who asked them here?"

"It was the natural thing to do," Frank said. "Robby was smart enough to see that."

"If we'd ignored them," Kelly said, "they'd have gone away."

"Sure they would," Robby said. "They'd have gone away wondering what we're so strange about, what have we got to hide. Then, when we kidnap Sassi Manoon—"

(27)

Frank said, "This way, they've been on our boat, they've seen we're just a bunch of harmless young guys on vacation, they won't give us another thought."

"That's right," Robby said.

Kelly knew it was right, though he was still reluctant to admit it. "Fish finder," he grumbled, turning away.

"It was all I could think of," Robby said. "I'm sorry. I didn't mean any disrespect."

"I know," Kelly said grudgingly. He shook his head. "All right, never mind. You were right, we had to let them come aboard. I just hope we don't have any more Nosey Parkers like that."

"Even if we do," Frank said, "we've got the perfect cover. Three young guys taking it easy at Montego Bay."

"I don't like a lot of people on my ship," Kelly grumbled. He looked at his watch, said to Frank, "You better get to the airport. She's going to land pretty soon."

"Right," said Frank.

"Remember," Kelly told him. "Pictures, facts, everything you can get."

"Right, Chief," Frank said, and saluted. Turning away, he began to gather his gear together—the camera, portable tape recorder, binoculars, light meter, each in its own leatherette case with its own strap to be put around his neck. When he was done, he had so many straps crisscrossing his chest he looked as though somebody had tried to cross him out.

Meanwhile, Kelly was saying to Robby, "Starnap wants background on Jamaica. Everything you can find. History, geography, laws, everything."

Robby nodded. "I know."

"Starnap also wants you to study the local citizens, learn to pass for one."

Robby smiled. "You mean I'm going to pass for colored?"

Kelly, who had no sense of humor, told him, "You're going to pass for Jamaican."

"Right," said Robby. "I'll see you later."

"I'll be here," Kelly said.

Frank and Robby left together, and at last Kelly was alone again on his ship. He felt irritable, the ship contaminated by so many presences for so long. Particularly the two snoops, that rotten Major and the woman with him. It would take him a while to get over that experience, no matter how necessary it had been to go through it.

In truth, Kelly knew that a lot of his edginess and irritability had nothing to do with Major Whatsisname and Miss Whosis at all, but were caused by the fact that the caper was actually under way. It was a frightening and exhilarating experience to move from the realm of theory to the realm of fact, so it seemed to him he could be forgiven if his reactions were a little extreme at the moment.

In a way he'd been disappointed when Robby and Frank had both agreed so readily to join him in this escapade. If one or both had refused, it would have necessitated a delay, perhaps of months. More planning, more waiting for a moment when Sassi Manoon would be vulnerable, more time spent searching for one or two partners. In a lot of ways Kelly would have preferred to be doing all that right now rather than sitting here in Montego Bay with two confederates actually out in the city at work on the plan.

Coming down here from Miami had been a kind of unexpected fun, though, the camaraderie of three contemporaries alone in the huge ocean, the sort of good time his college days had occasionally afforded, but the time since arrival had been nerve-racking in the extreme. And the unwanted visitors had been the last straw.

Well, he had some time to himself now, he could relax a bit, calm his nerves. He walked around *Nothing Ventured IV*, seeing all the familiar details of the ship, seeing that nothing was out of place, that the physical evidences of the extra two passengers were surprisingly slight. Robby and Frank had brought little luggage with them, and what possessions they had were now stowed mostly out of sight.

Kelly went last of all to the forward cabin. He switched on the light and gave Starnap a rueful smile. "My nerves are a wreck today," he said. He sat down at the console, flipped all Starnap's switches on, and the machine began to light up, banks of tiny bulbs flickering to life, a background hum beginning to fill the air.

"Well, now," Kelly said. "How about a little kalah?"

Kalah was a game, African in origin. Starnap was not properly organized to play a game like chess, but kalah, a mathematical board game with simple rules but infinite permutations, was an ideal sport to be shared by man and machine. Kelly and Starnap had wiled away many idle hours trying to outwit each other in that way, and it was with a feeling of almost nostalgic anticipation that Kelly now got out the kalah board and the seventy-two pebbles. "Best two out of three," he told Starnap, knowing full well they'd probably play half a hundred games before they were done.

(4)

Schweppervescence

Sassi Manoon, preceded by two golden Afghans on silver leads, stepped from the plane into the Jamaican sunlight and smiled beautifully down at all those camera lenses. "Stay out of the pictures, Benny," she said without moving her lips, too low to be heard at the bottom of the steps but loud enough for Benny, just inside the plane's doorway, to get every word.

She spent quite a while at the top of the steps, waving and smiling and posing for the photographers. This part of her life was only boring in retrospect, never while it was happening.

"This way, Sassi!"

"Wave, Miss Manoon! Thank you!"

"This way!"

"This way!"

"This way!"

"Christ," Sassi said, and kept on smiling, and came at last down the steps, the nervous Afghans leading the way, twitching their noses like thin dowagers suspecting something awful in the tea.

On the ground there was a sort of press conference:

"How long will you be here, Miss Manoon?"

"What's the word on you and Rick Tandem, Miss Manoon?"

"How does it feel to be a film festival judge, Miss Manoon?"

"What's your next feature, Miss Manoon?"

Sassi answered about half the questions, and ignored the rest. She liked to get attention from the press, but this was beginning to be ridiculous.

Colored policemen in short pants stood around in nervous paralysis, as though afraid any minute they'd be accused of impure thoughts. The background was full of gawkers gawking. The sky was huge and blue and cloudless, all the planes gleamed like the silver birds they're supposed to gleam like, and the humidity was enough to take the starch out of an ear of corn. Sassi found herself fading.

Benny Bernard was abruptly there, holding her elbow, saying to the reporters and photographers, "Okay, boys, that's all for now, boys, there'll be more tomorrow, boys, Miss Manoon is tired from her trip, boys, but she's happy to be here and she's sure it's going to be a grand festival."

Under her breath, Sassi said, "Good boy, Benny. Nice timing."

"Anything for Milady," Benny told her, steering a path for them through the crush.

A young man, painfully tall and painfully thin, was suddenly in the path. "Welcome to Jamaica, Miss Manoon," he said, sounding very British. "I'm Bullworth Spence, from Sir Albert. The car's this way."

Spence gestured, and followed his own gesture away. Sassi looked in bewilderment at Benny, who said, "Tell you in the car."

They followed Spence through the clamor to a black Rolls Royce. The Afghans and Sassi and Benny got in back, and Spence slid in beside the driver. A policeman shut the door after them and the car started slowly forward. A young photographer with a chest crisscrossed with straps took Sassi's picture through the side window, and then at last it was all behind them.

Sassi shook her head. "What was that all about? They practicing for De Gaulle?"

"You're hot stuff in the islands, lovey," Benny told her. "This place ain't blasé like LA and New York. Besides, those boys got to file some wordage to justify the old expense account."

"You know just what to say to make me happy, Benny."

Benny, not knowing when he was being lied to for ironic effect, took that straight. "Everything okay now, lovey?" he asked. "You not sore at me any more?"

"How could I be sore at you? Where are we going now?"

Benny looked forward, but there was a glass between the front and rear seats and they apparently couldn't be heard from up there. "You're the guest of Sir Albert Fitzroy during the festival," he told her. "That's his boy Spence up front with the cabby."

"I thought the festival was supposed to spring for a room."

"The studio arranged it this way," Benny said. "They thought it would be better."

"Bless the studio. What's a Sir Albert Fitzroy?"

"British. Head of United Kingdom Films. Also in tight with the government over there, on the board of this, board of that. You got nothing to worry about with him, he's a faggot."

"That's great."

"Anyway, you won't be around that much." Benny pushed an Afghan's head off his lap and took a notebook from his jacket pocket. "You want to hear the itinerary?"

"Might as well. And don't shove Kama around like that."

"Sorry." Benny opened the notebook. "Tonight there's a party in your honor in the Fitzroy house. Technically the host is United Kingdom Films."

"He wants me to work for him," Sassi said.

"Could be," Benny said. "I wouldn't know."

"I won't work for him," Sassi said. "I know that already."

"That's up to you," Benny said, still reading his notebook. "Tomorrow night," he said, "there's the official opening dinner. Then you're invited to—"

"When do I see movies? That's what I'm here for."

"Different page," Benny said, flipping to it. "Let's see. The first regular screening is tomorrow night, after the dinner. That's the British entry, *The Sun Never Sets*. I think it's an anti-war movie."

Sassi shivered. "All that blood," she said.

"But before that," Benny said, "there's two other movies you're going to see. Special screenings. One at—"

"How come?"

"Because you won't be here Friday. So you'll see Friday's movies tomorrow morning."

"Why?"

"Because you're a judge," Benny told her. "You've got to see all the movies."

"No, dummy. I mean, why won't I be here Friday?"

"Because you've got to be in New York for the opening."

Sassi frowned. "What opening?"

"Zzipp."

Sassi looked at him as though he was crazy. "Zip what?"

"Your movie," he told her. "The one with Rick Tandem. Opening in New York on Friday. Used to be *The Siren and the Scientist."*

"Oh," she said. "I thought they were calling it *Make Mine Madball.* That was the title after *Up Your Banners."*

"Well, now it's *Zzipp,"* Benny said. "I don't know what it'll be Friday. Anyway, because you won't be here Friday, you're getting special screenings tomorrow of Friday's movies. They're not bothering with the Blondie retrospective, unless you really want to."

"The what?"

"I didn't think you did." Benny consulted the notebook. "You view the Russian entry," he said, "tomorrow morning at ten thirty. It's called *The Boots of the Elk."*

"It's called what?"

"Schweppervescence," Benny told her. "You were the one wanted all this crap."

Sassi looked out the car window at all the poor people.

*

Frank, sounding very like Broderick Crawford, said into the

microphone, "Miss Manoon's in her car now, black Rolls
Royce, license plate BX 352. Still with the man and the two
dogs. Stupid-looking dogs."

The other reporters and photographers were milling
around the tarmac, drifting away, calling out to each other
with jokes of questionable taste. Frank headed for the
fence and his rented Vespa, saying into the microphone,
sounding now like Howard Duff, "The Rolls is leaving now.
You are following."

Bicycles and scooters dotted the roadway, the Rolls
rolling among them like a bishop in a kindergarten. Frank
hunched over the handlebars of his Vespa, the portable
tape recorder resting on his right hip, the slender
microphone clutched like William Buckley's pencil in his
right hand. The tape recorder was off now, and Frank
amused himself with his rendition of Otto Preminger
singing "Camptown Races."

One would think a man with Frank Ashford's talents
would be earning three hundred and twenty dollars a night
for the rest of his life on television, but one would be wrong.
In the first place, the great era of video vaudeville is sadly
behind us now, the outlets for jugglers, dog acts, mimics,
and plate twirlers decreasing year by year. In the second
place, it isn't enough merely to be able to talk like Cary
Grant, one has to be able to talk like Cary Grant saying
something funny. One needs an act, a routine, jokes, none
of which did Frank have.

Nor did he have a burning ambition to be another mimic
on TV. "Wasn't that wonderful, folks? Let's give Frank
Ashford a big hand!" As he himself had once said,
borrowing Winston Churchill's voice for the task, "I do not
consider that fit employment for an adult."

Unfortunately, he had as yet no idea what he wanted to do instead. Dealing in used comic books had been profitable enough, but his interest in it had paled when he'd attained his eighteenth summer—the people he was dealing with in that racket tended to be bores with tightly repressed sexual problems, and this, too, neither he nor Mr. Churchill considered fit employment for an adult.

From eighteen to twenty he'd occupied his time and mind and talents with failing the Army induction physical. They kept calling him back every three months and he kept injecting himself with things to make him fail. But this was a seasonal occupation at best, and not high pay, and he was just as pleased when the Army finally threw in the towel and gave him a permanent deferment.

• His Army career behind him, Frank struck off into greener pastures, and spent the next year and a half winning contests. He appeared on quiz programs, submitted entries to puzzle contests advertised in newspapers, sent his phone number to radio games and postcards to any company intending to have a drawing for anything.

But that, too, got boring after a while. Besides, a lot of the payoffs were year's supplies of this and that, and before long Frank's father's garage was full of soap, pudding, razor blades, detergent, and socks; Frank's father's car was exposed to rain and sun by the curb; and Frank's father was suggesting maybe it was time for the baby bird to emulate its big brothers and sisters and fly away from the nest. Also, the contest people get to know the professional winners after a while, and put their names on a list. Pretty soon Frank was being turned down for television quiz shows and his phone number wasn't being called any more and his postcard was no longer being drawn.

Now Frank was twenty-five, and for over three years he'd been drifting. His father was growing more insistent about the baby bird, even his mother was beginning to make nature noises, and Frank himself was beginning to think a place of his own might be nice. But where was the money to come from? How was Frank, without boredom, to support himself?

Until Kelly had come along, things had looked really grim. Frank had gone up to Walden Pond and lived in a shallow hole in the ground there for a while, but that had turned out badly, with a terrible head cold and nosy state troopers and a session with a state psychiatrist and all the rest of it, and his prospecting for gold in Death Valley had been even worse. Nobody replied to his application to become a pilot for PanAm, and though the CIA did respond to his application to them, it was only to ask his draft status, so that time *he* didn't respond.

But then, in the nick of time, along came Kelly. When Frank had first known Kelly a decade before, Kelly had been an EC nut, a collector of all the EC horror comics and science fiction comics. He'd even take a war comic, if it was EC, and he'd take science fiction comics even if they weren't EC. Ten dollars, twelve dollars, he hadn't cared what he had to pay for the early EC stuff, and for a while Frank had looked upon him as an unending source of income, but he hadn't expected Kelly ever to supply his income in any other way.

It had taken him a while yesterday to realize that down beneath Kelly's lunatic exterior there beat a brain of pure gold. If Kelly's scheme worked, and Frank was convinced it would, it was the answer to all his problems.

A mountain in Manitoba, that's what he'd buy, with a lake to land his seaplane on. And a town house in New York, facing Gramercy Park. With the comfort and time that two hundred eighty-five thousand dollars could give him, he could at last in a leisurely fashion make up his mind about what he intended finally to do with his life.

But right now there was the Rolls to consider. One drives on the left in Jamaica, and Frank found his Vespa had a tendency to veer rightward, like an aging West Point alumnus. This was bad enough on The Queen's Drive, the blacktop road leading down into town from the airport, but once in the middle of town on Fort Street, surrounded by Cortinas and Morris Minors, it became downright dangerous. Frank hunched over his handlebars and dogged the Rolls' tail.

The Rolls trundled through town and out Barnett Street —past the police station, which Frank was too troubled by traffic to notice—and completely out the other side of the city. Monstrous trucks and buses kept threatening to skin the knuckles on his right hand, and he was developing a squint in his right eye.

Finally, five miles from town, the Rolls turned leftward into a driveway that arched uphill past two stone columns and a lot of jungle flora up to a large white house with balconies. The house could barely be seen from the road, but all of Montego Bay could surely be seen from the house.

Frank overshot the driveway, stopped the Vespa beside a tree, leaned against the tree as he switched on his tape recorder, and said à la Jack Webb into the microphone, "Four-seventeen. Suspect car entered driveway of private residence at—"

"And this," Bullworth Spence announced as they entered the front hall of the house, "is Sir Albert Fitzroy!"

It was the first time Sassi had ever seen anyone introduced as though he were a natural wonder, but in this case the method was maybe appropriate. Sir Albert Fitzroy didn't look like a person so much as a three-dimensional painting of a person, standing there in the hallway with a broad smile on his face and his hand out in greeting. On seeing him, one felt like saying, "How lifelike!"

But he wasn't lifelike, not really, the way movies in Technicolor aren't really lifelike. His jacket was too perfect a blue, his trousers too totally wrinkle-free, his shoes far too silkily polished. The expansion band of his watch seemed to glisten with a life all its own, as did the small plain gold ring on his left pinkie. His hands and face were scrubbed to a pink and healthy glow never seen outside Norman Rockwell paintings, and his hair, black on top and gray at the temples, thick and glossy, was swept back from a broad forehead in an effect impossible to attain in real life. The smile was not too much and not too little, the jaw was firm, the cheekbones high, the face ruggedly handsome and admitting to perhaps forty-five, the eyes sincere and pleased and welcoming and way too honest to be believed.

Not really expecting this apparition to reply, or even to move, Sassi put on her coming-to-the-business-meeting smile and said, "I'm very pleased to meet you, Sir Albert."

"I have been looking forward to knowing you, Sassi. May I call you Sassi?"

The voice was perfect, just like everything else. A resonant baritone, rich and trustworthy. But it, too, was just too perfect. Sir Albert's voice reminded Sassi of those recordings made by celebrities who can't really sing, and in the final published record one can sense the ghostly presence of the technicians, all of the taping and retaping, splicing and resplicing, the filters and the mixing, the echo chambers and the adjusting of the treble and bass control, so that what comes out sounds as though it never was entirely human.

Sassi was so bemused by this voice, and by the fact that Sir Albert could move his head and his hand, like the Walt Disney robot of Abraham Lincoln, that it took her a second to realize she'd been asked a question. Could he call her Sassi. She said, "Of course, Sir Albert. I wish you would."

"Thank you, dear lady." And he kissed her hand, which she'd been sure he would do.

"This is Benjamin Bernard," she said. "My press secretary."

It was fascinating to watch. As the men exchanged greetings, Sassi saw the little mechanical eyes in Sir Albert's head flick at Benny, assess him, realize he was neither important nor homosexual, and cross him off the list. The eyes seemed to go out of gear, like a car shifting into neutral, and Sassi knew Benny would never really exist for Sir Albert ever again.

Sir Albert turned back to Sassi, saying, "You must be tired from your trip. I'll have you shown to your room, and you can freshen up. Come down any time, and if you want anything from the kitchen just dial seven on your telephone."

Another hotel. Sassi said, "Thank you very much, Sir Albert."

"And I hope you don't mind," the baritone rolled on, "but I've arranged a sort of welcoming party in your honor this evening. I hope you'll feel like coming."

"Benny told me about it," Sassi said. "I'm sure it'll be fun." Sure.

After very little more talk, Sir Albert turned them back over to Bullworth Spence— "You can think of young Spence here as an extension of my right arm"—who took them through a cool dim white room to the foot of a broad flight of stairs, where he turned them over to a silent slender Negro, who showed them upstairs to their rooms.

Sassi's windows faced the sea, an infinitely more beautiful view than Las Vegas, but she found it not much more pleasing. Even here she couldn't get away from the pressure.

She'd been right, the studio was angling to do a load-out. She was one of the last of the major stars still in a contractual situation with a Hollywood studio—her third analyst had said it was because she was looking for a father figure —and the contract still had two pictures to run, after which she intended to follow everybody else into free-lance work and maybe even her own production company. At thirty-two it was time for a girl to get over the need for a father figure.

At any rate, she had script refusal on her films, and she knew right now she wasn't going to be happy with any script shown her by Sir Albert Fitzroy. There was something too efficiently predatory about the man, she wouldn't be happy working for him, she could tell that already. And another thing she could tell already, Sir Albert wasn't the sort to offer the hospitality of his house just for the fun of it. This invitation had to be the opening move in an attempt to get her for some property he had in mind, and since the studio had okayed the arrangement, they must be planning to have her work off her last two pictures on loan-outs, probably in deals that would help the studio in a lot of other ways. And the hell with that. She'd work on the lot she knew, with the production people she knew, in the country she knew, or she wouldn't work.

But though she had no intention of working for Sir Albert, she couldn't just tell him to go fly a kite, she would have to wait and watch him on the surely roundabout route he would take before reaching her with a direct offer, and then she would have to refuse with regret, and let him try to persuade her, and continue to smile and be polite and regretful all the way through the goddam movie festival, spoiling the whole thing.

Why *couldn't* she just tell him no, right now? She was Sassi Manoon, wasn't she? She was rich and powerful and important. Why not tell him no and switch to a hotel and give herself a chance to enjoy the stinking festival? Why not?

Well, in the first place, there wouldn't be a hotel room this side of Fort Lauderdale, not during a major film festival. And in the second place, things aren't done that way. Things are done politely. The effect is the same, she would not be making a movie for Sir Albert Fitzroy, but the method is slower and infinitely more painful.

Usually, an affair like this wouldn't directly involve a meeting of the principals at all. A representative of Sir

Albert's, probably Spence, would contact Max Manning with the proposition, Max would offer it to Sassi, Sassi would say no, Max would say no, Spence would tell Sir Albert the answer was no, and Sir Albert would suggest a slightly different proposition instead. And so on. This way, Sir Albert was cutting out the middlemen, but the essential method would remain the same.

So she hadn't gotten away from her life at all, had she? And tonight's party should be a killer-diller, a huge garish bash full of boring people. Well, all she'd be expected to do was make a token appearance, somewhere around ten o'clock, and for the rest of the evening she could stay up here and read a book.

"That's wonderful," Sassi Manoon told the ocean. "That's really great."

(5)

Data

Pedaling his bicycle along Kent Avenue in the orange light of the setting sun, Robby gave himself over at last to brooding. There was nothing else to think about at the moment, so his thoughts turned to the black man's burden, which was himself, the fact of his color, the anomaly of his position in the world.

Never before in his life had Robby felt that anomaly as strongly as today, being an American Negro on the island of Jamaica. All day he had felt ghostly, unreal, like those spirits in fantasy stories who cannot make themselves heard by the living. The natives he had moved among could tell by his clothes and accent that he wasn't one of them, he was an American, his kinship was with the tourists; and the American tourists could tell from his skin that he wasn't one of them, he was a Negro, his kinship was with the natives. With both camps assuming him to belong to the other side, he had wandered all day in his own private no man's land, and whenever he had spoken to anybody he had felt as though his voice had an echo.

Not that things like that should bother him any more. Very soon none of that would matter at all, because he was going to have almost three hundred thousand dollars, and if there was anything on God's green earth that could equalize a black man in white society it was gold. Why else would he take a chance on a wild scheme like this?

Robert "Robby" Creswel, son of a Boston doctor and his receptionist/nurse/wife, graduate of a fine old New England polytechnical college, veteran of three years' peaceful duty in the Coast Guard, non-marcher, non-picket, non-sitter-in, had been a Negro all his life, and all his life he had believed that the only way to protect himself from the consequences of that fact was to somehow become a millionaire. Given enough money, he believed, a man could rise above any inconvenience, no matter how great.

Until Kelly had come along with this starnapping plan, Robby'd had no idea how to go about attaining that goal of wealth. He was adapted neither to be a boxer nor to go into show business. Any large corporation in America would have been delighted to have such a credit to his race for their token Negro executive trainee, but what future was there in that? No millions, that was for sure. So Kelly and Starnap had been manna from heaven.

Of course, the Sassi Manoon kidnapping wasn't a final answer in itself, but it was a damn good first step. A bright boy of any color with three hundred thousand dollars to invest can still do all right for himself, if he has a good tax lawyer. All Robby had to do was quadruple that original investment, and there was the million. After that, the money would take care of itself.

In the meantime, he was still naked in this world, he still suffered the slings and arrows of outrageous Caucasians, he still felt himself lost in the gulf between the planets when he moved around downtown Montego Bay, and while riding his rented bicycle back out to Kelly and the boat he still tended to fall into gloominess and brooding.

But he had news, he reminded himself, trying to cheer himself up. It didn't entirely work, he still felt gloomy, but at least the thought of how cheery the news would make Kelly and Frank eased his moroseness a little.

He dismounted from his bicycle at the entrance to the yacht club, left it leaning against the wall there, and went into the building, downstairs, out the other side, and along the dock to *Nothing Ventured IV*. He passed *Redoubtable* on the way, saw Major ffork-Linton and Miss Rushby sitting on deck to view the sunset, and was surprised when Miss Rushby smiled pleasantly and waved to him. "Lovely sunset," she called.

Robby hadn't noticed it. "Beautiful," he said, and smiled back, grateful for small acts of humanity and hating himself for being grateful. He walked on and noticed now that the sunset was indeed beautiful, the sky blue and purple and orange and red, the sea violet with a yellow-orange road leading straight to the red ball of the sun sitting on the far horizon. It made him smile, and for the moment forget his troubles.

Frank and Kelly were not on deck. Robby boarded the

ship and found them down in the main cabin, Kelly looking at slightly blurred photographs of Sassi Manoon at an airport. Frank was pointing, saying, "That guy came on the plane with her. They didn't seem to get along too well. I think maybe he works for her."

Kelly nodded, and looked at Robby. "How'd you do?"

"Fine. But I'll never get the Jamaican accent. It's kind of English, but different."

Frank, in a perfect Jamaican accent, said, "Mon, it's a distinctive sort of speech here on the islands."

"That's it," Robby said. "That's exactly what it sounds like. Every time I try it, I sound like Barry Fitzgerald."

"Well, work on it," Kelly said. "Anything else to report?"

Robby removed his portable tape recorder, sliding the strap over his head and putting the machine down on the coffee table. "Lots of stuff on there," he said. "Background material. And I got all these pamphlets and things," he added, pulling bright-colored brochures from all his pockets. "And I heard some gossip down in town," he said. "Sassi Manoon is staying at a house outside of town rented by Sir Albert Fitzroy, the big English movie producer."

"I followed them out there," Frank said. "Big house. White, two stories high, up on a hill. Very Spanish-Mexican-looking."

"They're having a party there tonight," Robby said. "A huge party with hundreds of people, with Sassi Manoon the guest of honor."

Kelly sat up, looking alert. "At the house? Where she's staying? A party?"

"Huge party," Robby told him. "Too big to tell if they've got gate-crashers or not."

(*48*)

Kelly jumped to his feet, rubbing his hands together. "The gods are smiling," he said. "This is a good omen."

"We must have a lucky star," Frank said, grinning. "Or anyway we're going to get one."

"And tonight we get to see her in the flesh," Kelly said. "*And* case the joint where she's staying. And maybe get a lot of valuable information. Robby, what time is this party?"

"It starts at eight."

"We'll get there at nine thirty." It was one of the few times Robby had ever seen Kelly smile.

(6)

Coming to Meet

The driveway curving up to the house was full of parked cars— here a Rolls, there a Cadillac, somewhere else an Alfa Romeo. The late arrivals were parking way down near the public road and walking up the slanting blacktop past the double row of amber lights hanging from the palms. White and amber spots shone on the front of the house, highlighting it against the darkness. Island music pulsed from somewhere inside.

Kelly and Frank and Robby got out of the cab at the foot of the driveway, paid the driver, and walked up to the open front door. All three were dressed in ties and sport jackets, and even Kelly looked festive for the occasion.

Other people were still arriving, and there was no one at the door to greet or challenge them. Kelly and Frank and

Robby strolled casually inside, nodded to one another, and separated, each heading for a different part of the house.

Downstairs, the house was full; upstairs, empty. Servants moved in and out of the kitchen, carrying trays of drinks, hors d'oeuvres, empty ashtrays. Guests moved, talked, laughed, munched, drank, tinkled ice cubes.

The older the guest, the closer to the front door he was likely to stay. The main living room, off the entrance, was full of the cigar smokers, the businessmen, the money boys; words like *probate* and *percentage* thudded off the white walls and buried themselves in the purple carpet. Some wives were there, too; fat-armed women expensively but uselessly dressed, sitting in a cluster like a display of joke dolls in a novelty shop, talking to one another about the quality of service in this hotel, that hotel, all over the uncivilized world. Amid them sat Miss Rushby, blending with the group like a submarine in a school of whales.

Deeper in the house, in what was called the library because it was full of books bought en masse at an auction, were the pipe smokers, the intellectuals, the established writers and directors, and here and there a creative producer, telling each other how crappy their agents were. The wives here tended toward straight hair and plain talk; some of them hadn't seen each other since the last march on Washington. In a corner, Major ffork-Linton was involved with five others in a game of liar's poker, and seemed to be so far the only winner.

Beyond the library, in what was called the solarium because it leaned heavily to windows and plants, were clustered the cigarette smokers, the pros, the actors and singers and comedians and personalities and celebrities, telling each other what great book jackets they'd read recently. Here the wives looked like audition day at the Copa— leggy, expensive, blank-faced. Benny Bernard, trying to do himself a little good, was looking around for a conversation to join.

Out by the pool were the pot smokers, the young hippies, the twenty to twenty-five crowd, the new breed— TV series regulars, rock group members, actors who were feeling guilty about copping out on La Mama because they were too young to have copped out on Circle in the Square and too old to have copped out on Yale. Nobody was married out here, or at least not very married, and everybody had already slept with everybody else, so there was nothing to do but dance around the pool and talk to one another— shouting over the music— about analysis.

Scattered through all the rooms, like the yeast in an up- side-down cake, were the critics, the magazine writers, the free-lance journalists and the book-compiling *aficionados* who fill the chinks and crannies of every film festival worthy of the name. These were the only guests talking about movies, and they were doing so passionately, knowl- edgeably, and interminably.

It was out by the pool that the band had been set up. Marimba,, electric guitars, drums, gourds, bongos— the boys in the band stood there and drove toward morning, pumping music out over the pink translucent pool. The pool had underwater lights, with red bulbs. Green spots shone on the palm trees by the bamboo fence at the edge of the property, blue and yellow circling disk lights shone on the faces and drinks of the dancers. Beyond the pool area lay the tropical night, black, heavy, alive with mosquitoes.

It was to the pool that Robby gravitated, moving like slender smoke through the house. The only Negroes inside the house were servants, but out back there were half a dozen Negro guests, and Robby relaxed at once. There was a surge of motion counter-clockwise around the pool, people dancing singly or in pairs— it was hard to tell which— and Robby forced his way into the jumble, found a tiny clearing, and began to frug.

Kelly joined the money men in the front room. Unobtrusively he sat in a corner, listening to the talk of mergers, proxy fights, realignments. Unobtrusively his pocket tape recorder spun within his jacket, the microphone wire leading to what looked very like a hearing aid in his left ear.

Into the solarium sidled Frank, slyly smiling, and amused himself by doing the voices of everybody in the room. People began to answer people who hadn't asked anything, and gradually a vast fog of confusion settled in, making everybody sore. As Frank sidled out again the room was well on its way to a mass fistfight.

Upstairs, sitting in a narrow cone of light from her bedside lamp, sat Sassi Manoon, the latest book from Bernard Geis open in her lap. On the table beside her were an ice bucket, a carafe of water, a bottle of Scotch and a glass, all half full, and so was Sassi. Though her room faced the front of the house and she had the air conditioner switched on full, she could still hear the pulsing beat of the band, pounding away down there as though they were trying to build a house before daylight.

Sassi was getting sloshed, and she didn't care. She knew she should go down and put in an appearance at the party soon, and she didn't care. She didn't even care that there was somebody knocking at her door, though when they just kept knocking she finally called, "Come in."

The door opened and the Spence character stuck his head in. Sassi was sitting up on the bed, but she was fully dressed, in orange stretch-pants and a white top. She squinted out of her cone of light at Spence in semi-darkness at the door and said, "What do you want?"

He came all the way in, smiling nervously. "Just wondering how you were, Miss Manoon. We haven't seen much of you downstairs."

"You haven't seen any of me downstairs," she said.

"Uh," he said.

"Fitzroy sent you?"

"Oh, no, Miss Manoon. I just thought—"

"Sure," said Sassi. "I'll be down in a little while."

"I just wanted to see if you were all right."

"I'm fine. The neighbors play the radio too loud, but other than that I'm dandy."

Spence frowned, bending forward at the waist. "I beg your pardon?"

"Nothing. Forget it. I'll be down in a little while."

"Yes. Well—all right. Yes. Just wanted to be sure—just checking to be sure —just checking to—" Babbling, Spence backed his way out of the room and shut the door behind himself.

"I hate Sir Albert Fitzroy," Sassi said aloud, and reached for her glass.

*

Out front, another cab had stopped, letting out a young lady named Jigger Jackson, a redhead wearing a shiny white plastic top and shiny yellow plastic mini-skirt and shiny white plastic flats. In her left hand she carried a tiny shiny white plastic purse, and she was not unaware that the cab-driver waited in order to watch her walk up the driveway toward the house. Not unaware, and not unpleased.

Jigger Jackson was twenty-one years old, and could vote for President if she wanted. But what she wanted was more important than that. What she wanted was to be a movie star.

Every film festival has them, they add a touch of transient beauty to the occasion, like bright-colored flowers at a lawn party. The film festival is the one place where the real world and the world of movies intersect, where producers and directors and actors and movie businessmen are all gathered together and accessible, and it isn't surprising that so many would-be stars have chosen to follow the circuit of the film festivals, making contacts, hoping for contracts, praying for the break.

Jigger Jackson was one of these. She had followed the film festivals for almost two years now, from Cannes to Venice, from Acapulco to Karlovy Vary, from Berlin to Moscow to New York to Locarno to San Francisco. She had been to the festival of underwater films held annually above water in Toulon, and the science fiction film festival in Trieste, and the sports film festival at Cortina d'Ampezzo, and even the Negro film festival in Dakar, Senegal. She had seen a lot of hotel rooms, some of them containing movie producers or at least people who said they were movie producers, and the words "screen test" had been whispered in her ear more than once, but up until the present moment no one had ever expressed an interest in seeing Jigger Jackson sign her name on a dotted line.

So Jigger had decided the time had come for a change. The trouble was, there was too much competition from other broads on the one hand and too much duplicity from festival-going men on the other hand, and so far as Jigger could see, the odds against her breaking through just weren't good enough to go on with it. What she needed was an entirely new approach, a new concept, and she thought she finally had one this time, she thought she'd really come up this time with the winning notion.

The thing was, all the girls trying their stunts at the film festivals—parachuting from rented planes onto the decks of private yachts, stripping in hotel lobbies, engineering minor automobile accidents with major stars—were aiming those stunts at *men*, hoping to attract the man's attention long enough to work a little sex appeal into a quid pro quo. But nobody, so far as Jigger knew, had ever tried working a stunt through a *woman*.

Not sexually, there were some things Jigger thought she probably wouldn't do for stardom, but sex wasn't everything, after all. And it had occurred to Jigger one thoughtful afternoon a few weeks ago that everybody likes a protégé, that it makes a successful person feel magnanimous and excellent to help a younger person up the ladder, that history was full of painters helping younger painters, successful writers encouraging beginning authors, and so on and so on. Why wouldn't a successful actress feel the same way? If Jigger were to go up to one of the really big-name movie stars and say, "Miss Soandso, you are my ideal, I'm trying to pattern my life on you, I see all your pictures, and I want to be in movies just like you," why wouldn't that big-name star feel touched and honored, why wouldn't she feel like helping Jigger make her dreams come true? Why not?

Jigger saw no reason why not, no reason at all. At the very worst, it couldn't hurt to try, and at the best she might have stumbled onto something brilliant.

Well, tonight was her first chance to test the theory, which was why she was crashing the party in honor of Sassi Manoon. If she could get Sassi Manoon to sponsor her in Hollywood, even a little bit, even just as far as a screen test and maybe an agent, that was all she'd need. After that, she was sure she could handle the rest for herself.

She strolled through the open front doorway of the house, ready with a series of lies if anybody challenged her, but no one paid her any attention at all. She saw how crowded the place was, and knew she was safe. Just so the joint wasn't so crowded that she never got a shot at Sassi Manoon.

She stopped at the first doorway on the right, looked in, saw all those gray hairs, smelled all that cigar smoke, heard someone say something six percent, and nodded to herself. "If I don't get anywhere with Sassi Manoon," she told herself, "I'll try my luck in there." She moved away from the doorway and deeper into the house.

*

Frank was dancing with somebody's secretary. That is, he was dancing in her general vicinity, and they'd agreed before starting that they would consider they were dancing this dance "together." They were talking about Sassi

Manoon as they danced, which was only natural since Sassi
Manoon was the guest of honor, even though it was now
nearly midnight and Sassi Manoon hadn't as yet put in an
appearance, and also because this girl here, somebody's
secretary, happened to have had a great deal to do with the
planning of Miss Manoon's Jamaican itinerary. She enjoyed
talking about it, and Frank enjoyed listening.

Robby was also in conversation, though not out by the
pool. He was in the kitchen, and he was talking to the villa's
houseman. The tenants came and went, every two weeks
or every four weeks, but the villa's houseman stayed on.
This was *his* house, regardless of the fact that the technical
ownership resided with a real estate combine in Kingston,
and he took a proprietary pleasure in discussing it. Robby
listened attentively, partly because he was truly interested
and partly because he could barely understand the
houseman's English.

In a far corner of the kitchen, handy to the booze,
slumped Benny. His attempts to do himself some good in
the solarium had come to nothing, Sassi Manoon's non-
appearance at her own party had made Sir Albert begin
glaring at Benny as though it was his fault and he could do
something about it, and all in all Benny had decided about
the only sensible thing for him to do was get smashed. He
was smashed.

In the library, Major ffork-Linton was thirty-five pounds,
seventy-five dollars, one hundred sixty marks and thirty-
two thousand four hundred sixty-one lire ahead at liar's
poker, which is pretty good since it is impossible to cheat
at liar's poker.

Upstairs, in a front sitting room, Miss Rushby sat at a card
table with three bridge-playing ladies cut from the pack

down in the living room. The lady to Miss Rushby's right cut the pack, which did her no good because it is possible to cheat at bridge, and Miss Rushby dealt out the first hand.

Constantly on the move through the house, smiling his Styrofoam smile and cursing the day Sassi Manoon was born, was Sir Albert Fitzroy. He had greeted every familiar face, introduced himself to those faces which while not familiar did look important, and seen to it that the mechanics of the party—food and drink and ashtrays and music— were kept going smoothly. But where was Sassi Manoon? The least she could do was put in an appearance, but no, not a whiff of her. Spence had reported her drinking and surly as of ten o'clock, so God alone knew what sort of condition she was in by now. Sensing a scene in the air if he approached her, he was staying downstairs, smiling, moving from guest to guest, hoping everybody was enjoying himself too much to remember there was supposed to be a guest of honor here.

The guest of honor, in fact, was asleep. Still in her orange slacks and white top, the Scotch now nearly gone from the bottle beside her, the bedside lamp still lit, her head bowed over the novel still open in her lap, Sassi Manoon snored faintly, at last relaxed.

Someone else who wondered when Sassi Manoon was going to show was Jigger Jackson, who had been at this party long enough by now to know it was typical of film festival parties and therefore unlikely to be useful to her in any way other than to effect a meeting with Sassi Manoon. But not if she didn't come out in the open.

There was a flight of stairs tantalizingly present, seemingly in the background wherever Jigger looked, and she knew Sassi Manoon had to be somewhere at the top of those stairs. Did she dare go up them? People did go up occasionally, when both downstairs bathrooms were in use, so she wouldn't be questioned or stopped. But once up there, what would she do? Just keep trying doors? Do the old "Oh, I thought this was the bathroom. Say, aren't you Sassi Manoon?"

Well, it was better than standing around down here being eyed by people's public relations men. No one on earth is hornier or less useful to a girl's career than a public relations man.

Enough. Nothing ventured, nothing gained. Jigger went upstairs.

The first room she tried was full of old biddies playing cards, and the look one of them gave her as she stuck her head in let her know she wasn't exactly welcome. The second was a bathroom. The third was a bedroom, pitch-black, and Jigger was about to shut the door again when she saw light flash in there, like lightning. But it couldn't be lightning, the sky was clear and full of stars.

Curious, always wanting to know about things and following her curiosity wherever it would lead her, Jigger slipped into the room and shut the door. The window across the way faced the side of the house, so there was very little light, but the blackness wasn't total. As her eyes adjusted, it was possible vaguely to make out the masses and shapes of furniture.

Light flashed.

There it was again! To her left, a small brilliant light, on and off in just a second, leaving a memory of whiteness on her retina, an impression of a desk under intense glare. It was like a flashbulb, only more confined in area.

Jigger squinted, trying to see. There was something, something—

A small sound. A tiny rustle of paper, soon ended.

Flash.

There was someone there. Jigger could make him out now, a darker mass against the general darkness of the room, standing slightly hunched over, in profile to her, doing something.

Rustle.

Flash.

A desk, it was a desk. There was something on the desk, papers of some kind, and he was turning the papers over, pages or whatever they were, turning them over one at a time and then shining that quick light—

Taking pictures.

Jigger had seen enough spy movies to know what this was all about. Clandestine skulduggery, microfilm cameras, high-speed directional flashguns, miniaturized spy equipment for the new miniaturized spy. And too involved in his work to have noticed her come in, the brief opening of the door impossible for him to see after watching the flashes of his own picture-taking after a while.

But here? In a movie producer's house? What kind of international secrets did movie producers know?

Rustle.

Jigger considered the question, *Am I scared?*

Flash.

No.

Rustle.

Why not?

Flash.

What's he going to do to me, that's why not. Besides its being a full house downstairs, whatever this guy is up to can't be all that serious, not here, not serious enough to make him do me any real damage.

Rustle.

And besides that, if I blow the whistle on him, maybe that puts me in good with my host, Sir Albert Fitzroy, the English movie producer.

Flash.

But let's not be too hasty. Let's find out what's going on first.

Jigger put out her hand to the light switch, and flooded the room with light.

Kelly fainted.

Jigger couldn't believe it. She'd turned the light on, the guy at the desk had jumped as though he'd had a heart seizure, the camera had gone spurting out of his hands, he'd stared at her wild-eyed through his glasses, and then his eyes had rolled upward disgustingly into his head, his mouth had gone slack, and he'd fallen over backward onto the floor.

Maybe it *was* a heart seizure. She hurried over, grabbed his wrist, and felt his pulse clicking away like the Florida Special when there's no strike on.

Well, that was good. She hadn't wanted to kill the poor bastard, just see him.

On the surface, Jigger displayed a hardness and callousness that was mostly defensive and partly wishful thinking. She wanted to be tough, but every now and then something would happen to sneak through that toughness and touch the humanity inside. Jigger had an Achilles heel. She couldn't help it, she was a sucker for a shnook.

And it was hitting her now. Kneeling there beside the fallen photographer, holding his wrist in her hand, looking at his slack-jawed unconscious face, she felt an encroachment of tenderness so unexpected and unwanted as to be downright embarrassing. His glasses had fallen off when he'd fainted, one lens was broken, and with those broken glasses beside his head, plus the little pontoon-shaped marks of spectacle-wearing on either side of his nose, he looked as defenseless and pathetic as a puppy dog.

"Shnook," Jigger said gruffly, trying to retain her equilibrium, but it was no good. She felt sorry for him.

Who was he, anyway? You can't keep calling the object of your pity *shnook*, it's inappropriate. Jigger, in an effort to effect a unilateral introduction, went through the shnook's pockets and found:

One recording apparatus, tape, pocket, Japanese manufacture

One watch, stop

One measure, tape, cloth

One thingamabob, electronic, tiny (with wires)

One lighter, cigarette, butane

One cigarette package, Lucky Strike green (back from war!), open

One ring, key (with keys)

One device, unidentified, black (with red buttons)

Three screws, metal, small

One kit, tool, plastic, tiny (contents: screwdriver regular, screwdriver Phillips, pliers, cutters wire, clamp, tube glue)

One wallet, leather, black

What a pile of junk. Jigger poked through it, picked out the wallet, and proceeded to get to know her new friend.

He wasn't exactly traveling incognito. Driver's license, boat registration, even a library card from Glen Cove, Long Island. The name on all these documents was Kelly Bram Nicholas IV.

Could that name possibly be an alias? No, that name could not possibly be an alias.

There was nothing in Kelly Bram Nicholas IV's wallet to explain all those odd items in his pockets. He seemed to be merely an average young guy, a few years older than herself, who had a boat and liked to read books from the library and liked to take pictures in darkened bedrooms in other people's houses. With nobody there.

All right, of what was he taking these pictures? Maybe that would explain things.

Jigger got to her feet and went over to the desk and found a small notebook open upon it. The camera, an incredibly compact Japanese contribution to international understanding, was lying on its side nearby, next to the miniature flashgun.

Jigger picked up the notebook, leafed through it, and found it to contain somebody's itinerary for the eleven days of the film festival. What movies to be seen and where, what parties to attend, what lunches, what meetings, everything. But whose itinerary?

There was no name in the notebook, but it had to belong to whoever was staying in this room. Jigger searched desk and dresser and closet, found nothing but anonymous male clothing with Los Angeles labels, and paused to consider whether the body on the floor could be the legitimate tenant of this room. But why take pictures in the dark in his own room? Why faint like that?

On the closet shelf she spied a suitcase, expensive-look-

ing. On the off chance, she pulled it down and opened it.
It was empty, but attached to the handle was a laminated
identification sticker reading: "B. B. Bernard, J-K Films,
Hollywood, USA."

B. B. Bernard? Jigger squinted, deep in thought. If he
came from Hollywood, USA, B. B. Bernard should be
known to her. J-K Films, of course, she knew all about, but
B. B. Bernard? Hmmmmmmm.

Thinking, going through one of the file drawers in her
head, she suddenly noticed the shnook. No longer asleep,
he was lying now on his back with his head slightly raised,
and was blinking. Open, his eyes had the unfocused look
of underdone poached eggs, but with blue yolks.

Jigger shut the file drawer in her head, walked over to
the bed, and sat on the foot of it. "Okay, buster," she said,
unconsciously going into her Humphrey Bogart number.
"Talk fast."

He had a terrible squint. "My glasses," he said, sitting up.

"On the floor there," she said, pointing. "They're bus-
ted."

He was blind as a bat. After he'd patted the floor vaguely
for a while, not finding the glasses, she finally went over,
picked them up, and put them into his waving left hand.
He put them on, recoiled from the jagged ruin of glass
directly in front of his left eye, shut that eye, looked at her
balefully with the other, and said, "What are you doing
here?"

It wasn't a bad bluff, as bluffs go, but Jigger wasn't
buying. "I'm taking pictures of B. B. Bernard's notebook,"
she said.

He reacted nicely, jumping a foot in the air, opening the
eye behind the broken glass, looking around frantically,

getting pale, the whole thing.

Afraid she'd overdone it and he'd pass out again, Jigger said soothingly, "It's okay, I didn't blow the whistle on you. Not yet, anyway."

He stopped gaping around, looked at her again, and finally caught hold of himself. "This isn't your room either," he said. "You're up to something yourself."

"Elementary, my dear Watson. I thought this was the bathroom. I walked in, I found you taking those pictures, and I screamed."

Worry showed in the open eye, the other one being closed again. "You screamed?"

"Not yet," Jigger said.

It took him a few seconds to get it, and then he said, "Why won't that work backwards? *I'll* do the hollering. Your word against mine."

"I'll tell them to search us both," Jigger said. "All they'll find on me is me, but on you—" She gestured toward the little pile of goods on the floor.

He saw it, patted his pockets, and became outraged. "You picked my pockets!"

"Everything's there," she said. "I wanted to know what name to call you. That's a lot of funny stuff you've got there, Kelly Bram Nicholas Four. You the TV repairman?"

"Yes," he said. Stuffing things into his pockets while he sat on the floor, he said, "That's exactly what I am." He was being very irritable.

"Sure," she said. "Give me a fast good reason why I shouldn't go over to that door there and scream."

He didn't have a fast good reason. Looking at her with his good eye, his expression twisted all out of shape, he said only, "Uhhh. . ."

"That's what I thought," she said, and got to her feet.

She got halfway to the door when he said, "I'm a reporter."

She turned and looked at him. "You're a what?"

"A reporter," he said, with more assurance. "I'm looking for a scoop."

"Make mine vanilla," she said, and headed for the door again.

"Wait!"

The desperation in that cry stopped her once more, and when she looked at him she saw he'd yanked his glasses off and was staring blindly in her general direction. That old maternal urge cropped up again, but she put a lid on it and sat on the lid. "What?" she said.

"I can't think," he said, as though being unable to think both enraged and terrified him. "I can't think without my glasses."

"You've still got one good eye."

"That's worse than—I keep opening the other eye and— I can't—I can't *do* it!"

He was really getting shook up. She went back and leaned down and automatically reached out and put her hand on his cheek, saying, "Easy, tiger, easy. Calm down a little."

His face jerked away from her hand at first, but then it stayed where it was, letting her touch him. The skin was as rigid as an automobile fender, but warmer. "I have more glasses back at the boat," he said. "Another pair."

"You want me to help you? Take you back to your boat?"

"Yes."

"Sure thing," she said. "As soon as you tell me what this spy jazz is all about."

"Spy—?" He blinked upward with blind innocence.

"Come on, chum. The pictures. How come you're taking pictures in B. B. Bernard's notebook?"

He shook his head, clenching his jaws together. Jigger felt the cheek muscles grind beneath her hand.

She straightened again, breaking contact, putting both hands on her hips. "You're in a bind, Charley," she said. "You'll be telling somebody, sooner or later. You want to tell me, or you want to tell B. B. Bernard?"

"There's nothing to tell," he said stubbornly. He was staring into the middle distance, beetle-browed.

"All right," she said. "Get ready for a good scream."

She'd barely turned away again when he said, quickly, "There are others involved. I can't take the responsibility, I can't say a word."

She looked back at him. "What others?"

"They'll be at the boat," he said, staring blindly upward and a little to her left. "Take me to the boat. If they say it's all right, then I'll tell you."

Jigger considered. This one on the floor here, this Kelly Bram Nicholas IV, wasn't a dangerous type, that was obvious, and if he was the one sent on the missions, what could the ones back at the boat be like? And she was more and more curious. What was going on here? And was there anything in it for her?

"Okay, buster," she said. "On your feet. I'll take you to your boat."

(7)

Jigger Bound

"He isn't there," Frank said. He and Robby were walking along the deck toward the boat, in which no light was shining.

"Maybe he's asleep," Robby said.

"Kelly? Now?"

"I guess not."

They'd waited at the house, turning down the Major's half-hearted offer of a ride back, but Kelly just hadn't showed up, and when at last the party was down to themselves, a few unconscious drunks, and the servants, they'd given it up, called a cab, and come back to the boat. Which was in darkness.

Or was it? They both saw it at the same time, a small light flickering palely on the boat, moving this way and that, then disappearing.

"A flashlight," Robby whispered.

"Something's up," whispered Frank.

They crouched, and tiptoed through the darkness toward the boat. Occasional boards creaked beneath their feet, but boats were creaking on both sides of them, so their own small noises disappeared in the general muffled hubbub.

The *Nothing Ventured IV* was broadside to the dock, with a gangplank canted up to the forward deck. Frank and Robby moved cautiously up this gangplank, crossed the deck, and went silently down the steps into the main cabin.

The flashlight was behind them now, in the forward cabin under the deck they'd just crossed. In with Starnap. Frank and Robby inched their way to the open door.

Frank peeked around the edge, and in there he saw a girl with red hair, a shiny white plastic top, shiny yellow plastic mini-skirt, and shiny white plastic shoes, bending over Starnap, studying it with the aid of a shiny chrome pencil flash.

The light switch was just inside the door. Frank hit it, the light came on, and the girl jumped, her pencil flash bouncing off Starnap and landing on the floor. "Okay," Frank said, stepping into the room, and the girl lammed him across the side of the head with her tiny shiny white plastic purse. Frank careened away into a wall and the girl ran out of the room and into the arms of Robby.

Frank came blundering back through the doorway, hurried past Robby and the girl, who were spinning around like a mechanical toy from Hong Kong, opened a drawer in the utility wall, and took out a pistol. It was unloaded, merely a possible prop in the kidnapping, but she wouldn't know that. He turned around, pistol in hand, and shouted, "Cut it out!"

The toy from Hong Kong continued to spin a few seconds

longer, till both parties spotted the gun, and then it ran down. The girl stood panting and glaring, and Robby reeled over to collapse on the sofa, saying "Whoosh!"

"Now," Frank said, turning on lights, keeping the gun pointed at the girl, "we'll find out what's going on around here."

"You think so," said the girl, breathing hard, partly from rage.

Frank said to Robby, "Get her purse."

She didn't want to hand it over, but with Frank holding the pistol on her, she didn't think she had any choice. She slapped it bitterly into Robby's hand when he came panting over to get it from her. "If you don't mind," she snapped, "I'll sit down now."

"Go right ahead," Frank told her.

She sat, folded her arms, crossed her legs, and sourly watched Robby go through her purse.

"Hmm," said Robby, and held up so Frank could see them Kelly's glasses. "Kelly's glasses," he said.

Frank looked at the glasses, then at the girl.

"One lens broken," Robby said.

Frank returned the girl's glare, saying, "What have you done with Kelly?"

"I'll trade you," she said.

Robby said, "Trade what?"

"I've got your buddy," she said. "You tell me what you three are up to, I'll tell you where he is."

"You'll tell us first," Frank said threateningly, "if you know what's good for you."

"Don't make me laugh," she said. "You three are about as dangerous as a flea act."

Robby said, "Maybe you'd like to talk to the police."

"And maybe you wouldn't," she said. "I caught your buddy taking pictures of somebody else's notebook in Sir Albert Fitzroy's house. You want me to start talking to the cops?"

Frank and Robby looked at one another. Robby said, "What now?"

"I don't know," Frank said, and something thudded.

Hushed, Robby said, "What was that?"

The something thudded again, and one second later the girl was off and running, trying for the stairs. Robby tackled her in mid-flight, Frank ran around them like a referee at a wrestling match, and in the middle of it all the something thudded again.

They got her off the floor at last, and back into the chair she'd started from, and Frank stood directly in front of her, pointing the gun at her nose. Breathing hard, he said, "It's in the bathroom, Robby, take a look."

Robby went over and opened the bathroom door, and in there was Kelly, bound and gagged and sitting on the toilet. "It's Kelly!" he shouted.

Frank smiled thinly at the girl. "So much for the trade," he said.

She folded her arms and glowered at the opposite wall.

Robby went into the bathroom and removed Kelly's gag. Kelly immediately began to babble: "There's a girl, there's —watch out for her—there's a girl, she knows, she's been—"

"We've got her," Robby said. He was untying Kelly's wrists.

"You've got her?"

"We've got her," Robby said, and untied Kelly's ankles. "Can you walk?"

"I think so." Holding Robby's hand, Kelly hobbled out

to the main cabin. "Glasses," he said. "In the drawer under Starnap."

"I'll get them," Robby said, and hurried away.

The girl said, "Starnap? What's that?"

Blinking blindly around, Kelly said, "Is she tied up? Don't let her get away."

"Don't worry," Frank said. "We've got her."

Robby came back with the glasses and fitted them to Kelly's face. Kelly blinked two or three times, shook his head, looked around, and said, "Right."

Robby said, "What happened?"

"No time for that now," Kelly said. "We have to feed the new information into Starnap."

"What about her?"

"Lock her aft. She knows too much, we'll have to keep her."

Robby said, "You mean, take *two* of them?"

"Can't be helped," Kelly said briskly. "We let her go, she'll ruin everything."

"Wait a second," the girl said. "You can't—"

"Lock her aft," Kelly repeated. "Then we've got work to do." Rubbing his hands together in workmanlike anticipation, he went forward to see Starnap.

"That's kidnapping!" the girl shouted.

Frank smiled at her. "Is that what it is? Think of that, Robby. We're kidnappers."

"Think of that," said Robby.

(8)

Caper

"But it's so soon," said Robby, sitting there with a piece of toast in his hand.

"Starnap says this morning," said Kelly, "and Starnap's running this operation."

"Let's hear it for Starnap," said Frank.

The three of them were sitting around finishing breakfast— bacon and eggs and toast and coffee. They'd been up all night, feeding Starnap the new information and receiving their orders, but they were all too keyed up to feel tired. Outside, a beautiful morning swelled like a balloon, Montego Bay sparkling and gleaming as though it had just had its teeth brushed.

"It just seems so soon," said Robby. "Maybe we ought to watch her some more first."

"Starnap," said Kelly, "says we know all we need to know. If we wait, other elements could come in and change things. Maybe after the first day she'll quit the festival and go back to Hollywood. Maybe the festival will shut down. Maybe somebody else will show up to take her around everywhere and make it too tough for us to pull the job at all. All sorts of things could happen."

"It's just so soon," said Robby. "That's all. It's kind of sudden. I'm willing, I just didn't think it would be this sudden." He finished his coffee.

Kelly looked at his watch. "Time to go," he said.

"I have to get my uniform," Robby said. He got up and went over to the door to the aft cabin, turned the knob, and said in surprise, "It's locked."

They all remembered at the same time. They stared at one another, and Robby said, "The girl."

"I completely forgot about her," said Frank.

"Hell," said Kelly. "All right, never mind her. She's safe there till we get back."

Robby said, "We have to give her breakfast, Kelly."

"Damn," said Kelly. Irritated, he went over and unlocked the door, looked in at the girl sitting on the bed in there, and said, "Come out here and eat your breakfast."

She turned her head and gave him a look of infinite scorn. "Don't mind about *me,*" she said.

"Good," said Kelly, on whom sarcasm was wasted, and shut her in again.

But then she pounded on the door so much they had to give her breakfast after all.

*

(75)

From the new Rose Hall development up in the hills along the coast to the east of Montego Bay there's a beautiful view of the Caribbean Sea, blue and gleaming under the huge dome of washed-blue sky, dominated by the sun.

Rose Hall is no Levittown. The plots are large and hilly, the houses are all architect-designed, the road curves gracefully through the tract. Many of the plots have been sold, but only a few houses are completed, each with its swimming pool, air conditioning, patio, privacy fence, and lush landscaping. Money lives on Rose Hall's hills, and more money is on its way.

An artist would love Rose Hall's view, and a sociologist would love its implications, but Kelly was neither. "It's up here someplace," he said, frowning at the undeveloped plots. "A purple garage door." Among the items his tape recorder had picked up last night from the moneyed conversations around him had been one about a house that would be empty up here today, its owner off to Kingston.

"Maybe they were drunk," Frank suggested. He was in the back seat, and Robby was driving. They were all in a pale blue Ford Cortina, an English car rented this morning from Avis.

"They kidded him about it," Kelly said. "It was serious. You heard the tape. A purple garage door."

"There!" shouted Robby, the car veering as he took one hand off the wheel to point. He was having trouble with this car; not only was he supposed to drive it on the left side of the road in Jamaica, the steering wheel was on the right, and the gear shift was on the left side of the steering wheel. That wouldn't have been so bad except there was another lever on the right side of the steering wheel, where the gear shift would normally be, only this one was for the directional signals. Robby had a tendency, whenever he wanted to shift into second, of signaling instead for a left, which confused him almost as much as it did the traffic behind him. But things were better now up here in Rose Hall, mostly because there was no other traffic and it didn't matter which side of the road he drove on.

The house at which he'd pointed, other than the purple garage door, was quite good-looking. A kind of extravagant ranch-style, it was constructed on stilts out over a slope falling away behind it toward the sea. Built crossways along the slope, it looked as if it would boast sea views from every room. Its stucco exterior was white; the rich landscaping around it was mostly green and red; the privacy fence around the swimming pool on its left side was of pale bamboo; and the carriage lamp beside the drive was sensible black and white. In company with all this the purple garage door, wide enough for a Piper Cub, looked like a huge bruise.

"What if he decided not to go?" said Robby.

"He said he had to be in Kingston today," Kelly said, "to meet his family. The other one said he'd pick him up at eight o'clock and take him to the airport. It was definite."

"Unless they were drinking too much," Frank said. "The guy could be in there asleep right now."

"We'll find out," Kelly said.

Robby had stopped the car on the road, near the driveway entrance. Now Kelly got out and walked up the driveway and along the slate walk to the front door. He rang the bell, waited, knocked on the door, waited, rang the bell again, waited, knocked on the door again, waited, shouted,

"Hello!" waited, rang the bell a third time, waited, shrugged and came back to the car. "Nobody home," he said. "Come on up."

"Okay," Robby said. As Kelly walked back up the driveway, Robby signaled for a left and raced the engine. "Damn," he said, switched the directional signal off, used his left hand to shift into reverse, and backed up. Then he signaled for a right and backed up some more. "Damn!" he said.

"You're doing fine," Frank told him.

"Shut up," Robby suggested. He switched off the directional again, shifted into first with his left hand, and drove the car up the slight slope of the driveway, stopping in front of the purple garage door.

In the meantime, Kelly had taken out a huge key ring containing many hundreds of keys and had started trying them, one after the other, in the lock in the middle of the purple face of the garage door.

Robby fiddled with the directional signal, took his foot off the clutch, and the car leaped forward and stalled. "*Damn!*" said Robby.

"You're a menace," Frank told him. "Let me out of here." He climbed out.

"Wait'll *you* drive it," Robby snapped. "Just wait."

Kelly kept trying keys.

"Time for my first metamorphosis," said Robby, getting out of the car and taking off his pants.

"There!" said Kelly. The garage door slid up and out of sight, which immediately made the house look a thousand times better. Inside was a sand-colored Mercedes-Benz 300. "Beautiful," said Kelly.

Robby had opened the rear door of the Cortina and taken out a pair of black trousers, which he now slipped on. He was already wearing a white shirt, to which he affixed a black bow tie, then shrugged into a thin black jacket. For the last, he put a black chauffeur's cap on his head. "How do I look?" he said.

Frank, à la Jack Benny, said, "Well, I don't know, Rochester. I may need the car myself later on."

Kelly had gone into the garage and opened the driver's door of the Mercedes. Sitting behind the wheel, he was trying various keys in the ignition. Robby walked in and stood on the cement beside him and said, "How is it?"

Kelly gave him a quick glance, said, "Fine," without really seeing him, and tried some more keys.

"See you boys later," Frank called, and got into the Cortina.

Robby, standing in the garage beside the Mercedes, watched Frank. He saw Frank adjust the seat, insert the key, start the engine, and signal for a left. Robby started laughing. Faintly he could hear Frank cursing. The directional light went off, and a few seconds later the Cortina rolled backward down the driveway.

The Mercedes started with a roar. "There!" shouted Kelly. He shut the engine, took the right key off the ring, got out of the car, and handed the key to Robby. "We're set," he said.

*

With the heel of her shoe, Jigger tapped out Morse code on the metal porthole cover:

(*79*)

SOS

SOS

SOS

"Damn," she said, gave it up at last, and flounced onto her bed. How was she going to get out of here? Wasn't there anybody around? What about the people in the next boat, couldn't they hear her?

The people in the next boat, had they been home, might in fact have been able to hear the tapping, but the people in the next boat—Major Alfred ffork-Linton and Miss Adelaide Rushby—were out.

*

Frank parked the Cortina in the parking lot of Mahoe Bay Hotel, shut off the engine, and just sat there a minute till the trembling went away. "Never again," he muttered. He then got out of the car with a feeling perhaps comparable to that of someone getting out of Wormwood Scrubbs, shut its door with more than necessary force, gave the car a dirty look it didn't deserve—it wasn't the car's fault if he wanted to drive on the right, sit on the left, and shift with his right hand—and walked away toward the hotel.

Mahoe Bay Hotel, like many of its sister hotels along the coast, was all in pieces. Its main building, a free-form airy whatsit two stories high, contained little beyond the desk, administrative offices, bar, a shopping mall, and some meeting rooms upstairs. The outdoor dining room was beyond that, near the swimming pool, and for the rest the hotel consisted of concrete cottages painted in pastels, each containing four units, all scattered here and there around a palm-dotted plain beside the sea.

Frank, for reasons not even known to himself, had decided to be Bud Collyer being Clark Kent. Going to the desk, he used Collyer's voice to say, "Hello, there. I'm from the Festival Committee. Where's the screening room?"

The clerk, a young lady with a blank expression, blinked slowly and said, "Beg pardon, sir?"

"Where they show the movies," Frank said.

"You mean a cinema?"

"I mean," Frank said, with Bud Collyer's Clark Kent patience, "the place in this hotel where Sassi Manoon is going to be watching a moving picture in"— he checked his watch—"forty-five minutes."

"In the hotel here?"

Frank sighed. "You don't own this place, do you?" he asked.

"What?"

"I mean, you work for somebody else, don't you?"

She nodded slowly, doubtfully.

"Good," Frank said. "May I speak with him or her?"

"Who?"

"Your employer."

"You want the manager?"

"Please," Frank said. "For the love of God."

"All right," she said agreeably, and went through a door and out of sight.

Frank waited, tattooing his fingertips on the formica.

The young lady returned, with another young lady, who looked at Frank with some suspicion and said, "The manager isn't in right now. May I help you?"

"Hard to say," said Frank. "I'm from the Film Festival

Committee, and I would like to see the place where the pictures that move like magic will be shown on the wall for Miss Sassi Manoon."

"You mean the screening room?"

"Yes," said Frank. "That's wonderful. The screening room, that's what I meant."

"Around that corner," she said coldly, "and through the second door on your left. Up the stairs, down the corridor to your right. Fourth door on the right."

"Thank you so much," said Frank.

"By the way," she said, still cold. "We don't appreciate racial slurs in Jamaica."

"Oh," said Frank. "I didn't know that."

"Try and remember it," she said.

"I will," said Frank. "I definitely will."

*

Kelly fingered the Persian carpet hanging on the wall. "This one, I think," he said. It was nine feet by twelve.

The salesman, an India Indian, smiled politely and rubbed soft hands together. "An excellent choice," he said.

"And it can be delivered now?"

"This very moment," the salesman said.

"Good. It would be hard to find my house otherwise. This way, your truck can follow me out there."

"Excellent," said the salesman.

The checkbook that Kelly took from his pocket now was certainly legitimate, and Kelly had no doubt that its owner really did have all that money in a Kingston bank. Of course, if the owner had checked his car's glove compartment this morning, from which Frank had rifled the checkbook outside Sir Albert Fitzroy's place last night, and if he had already reported his loss to the bank, and if the salesman checked with the bank before Kelly left the store, there might be a sticky moment or two, but with the amount of drinking done at last night's party, he felt pretty safe on the first two ifs and the obsequiousness of the salesman encouraged him to feel safe also on the third.

The encouragement was not false. The salesman took the check Kelly wrote—for three hundred twenty-seven pounds six shillings fivepence—with all the innocent joy of a yokel taking title to the Brooklyn Bridge. "I will have the carpet rolled," he said, "and placed at once within our van."

"I'll wait in my car," Kelly said. "The Mercedes out front."

"Of course," the salesman said, smiling and bowing. "I saw you drive up."

Kelly was sure he had. A chauffeur-driven Mercedes commands the right kind of attention, and the man in the back seat of same commands the right kind of belief.

"In just a moment, then," the salesman said, and Kelly returned his smile and went outside and got into the back seat of the Mercedes. Robby, behind the wheel, was sitting at attention, looking straight ahead, both hands on the steering wheel. The engine was running.

"Turn the engine off," Kelly said. "We look like we're ready for a getaway."

"Air conditioner," Robby said. "Engine off, air conditioner off. It gets hot in here."

"Oh," said Kelly.

Still facing forward, Robby said, "How'd we do?"

"Fine," Kelly said. "Just the way Starnap said."

"Starnap," Robby said, "has a very devious mind."

"Here they come," said Kelly.

Out of the driveway between the buildings came a Volkswagen Microbus, the big boxy one, painted a pale green. White letters on both sides said: MONTEGO BAY CARPET AND UPHOLSTERY COMPANY LTD. *Fort Street, Montego Bay.*

Kelly nodded through the rear window at the driver of the VW, who nodded back. There were two men in the VW, both Negro, both sturdy-looking.

Robby pulled away from the curb, and they drove eastward out of the city.

The Cortina was there, parked at the curb just beyond the driveway. Frank was nowhere in sight. "Good," said Kelly.

Robby drove the Mercedes up to the purple garage door and stopped. He and Kelly got out their guns— unloaded, but that was their secret— left the Mercedes, and walked back to the VW, which had stopped behind them. The driver and the second man had gotten out and were standing together beside the truck or bus or station wagon or whatever that kind of Volkswagen is. Kelly and Robby showed them their guns, and Kelly said, "Stick em up."

The two men looked at the guns in patent disbelief, and failed to raise their hands.

Robby said, "Hande hoch. Elevette les mains. Manitas arriba. What language do you two speak, anyway?"

"English," said the driver. "What's going on?"

"Highjack," Robby told him. "That's English."

The men looked at each other. The driver said, "It is?"

The purple door rolled up, and Frank came walking out to the sunlight, in blackface. Also in black hands. Also in a black wig.

Kelly looked at him and said, "You do Jolson once and we run the caper without you."

Frank looked sad.

The two men looked at Frank, and one of them said something fast to him in dialect. Kelly said to Robby, "What did he say?"

Robby said, with a touch of irritation, "How do I know? I'm from Boston."

"Why don't you ask me?" Frank said. He used his own voice.

The two men still didn't have their hands up. Kelly was getting mad. "Are you two going to put your hands up," he demanded, "or are we going to have to shoot you down like dogs to teach you a lesson?"

The driver said, "Don't you want the rug?"

"I'm going crazy," Kelly said.

Robby said, patiently, "Listen, fellows. This is what's going to happen. We're going to steal your truck. You're going to be—"

"Oh, no you're not," said the driver. "I have deliveries today. You'll get me in trouble with—"

"Crazy," Kelly said.

"You're not going to get in trouble," Robby said. "You're going to be tied up and left in the garage there. We'll let people know where you are this afternoon."

"Tie us up?" said the second man. "What do you mean, tie us up?"

(85)

"Tie you up," Robby explained, "as in tie you up. With rope. And gag you. Then we're going to take your truck away—"

"For nefarious purposes," put in Frank.

"But you people are American," said the second man. "You don't need our truck. Americans have all the money in the world. You don't have to take our truck."

"That's right," said the driver. "This truck is all we have, but you people have the Empire State Building, and Pan American Airlines, and—"

"And the New York Central Railroad," said the second man. "And Wall Street."

Kelly was getting mad. "You two put up your hands!" he shouted. "I'm sick of this! You just put up your hands, and do it this minute or you won't get tied up at all!"

"Good," said the second man. "I don't want to get tied up."

"I mean you'll get shot," Kelly said.

"You wouldn't shoot us," said the driver.

Kelly began to look wild-eyed. The hand with the gun in it started to tremble.

The driver said, "Wait a second." He was becoming alarmed.

Frank, employing Randolph Scott, said, "Better hoist those hands, partners. When Baby Face Preble gets his dander up, they's no stopping him."

The driver, still a bit doubtful, raised his hands. The other man hesitated a few seconds longer, but then he shrugged and raised his hands too.

"Good," said Kelly. He was breathing hard. "Now," he said. "March into that garage."

"You fellows can get in trouble for this," the driver said.

"No more argument!" Kelly snapped. "Get in there!"

The driver shrugged. "All right," he said. "But don't say I didn't warn you." He and the second man walked on into the garage.

*

Frank said, "It's on the second floor, all the way down the hall from the stairs."

Robby said, "No elevator?"

Frank said, "It's only two stories high, they don't need an elevator."

Robby said, "I was thinking about the rug."

Kelly said, "What's in the rooms around it?"

Frank said, "Men's room past it, the only other thing before the end of the hall. Conference room this side, small, got a round table, half a dozen chairs. Big conference room and broom closet across the hall."

Kelly said, "What's the chance of people in those rooms?"

Frank said, "Men's room, who can say? But none in the conference rooms."

Kelly said, "How do you know?"

Frank said, "I remembered the numbers of those rooms. Twenty-five and twenty-eight. Downstairs by the desk there's a notice board, says what meeting is where at what time. The smaller conference room has nothing scheduled all day, and the bigger one has nothing till three o'clock this afternoon."

Kelly said, "All right. What about the projectionist? In the room with her?"

Frank said, "No. There's two doors in there, almost right next to each other. They're marked twenty-seven and

(87)

twenty-seven A. Twenty-seven lets you into the screening room, twenty-seven A lets you into the projectionist's booth. There's a high step up just inside the door."

Kelly said, "Any way from the projectionist's booth into the screening room?"

Frank said, "No. Only out to the hall and in the next door."

Kelly said, "How big's the booth?"

Frank said, "Maybe five by eight. Really cramped. The two projectors are on the two sides, with the clear space in the middle. There's a folding chair there, and a table top that lets down from the wall. When it's down, two people in there wouldn't be able to get past each other. Up above it there's a sliding-door peephole into the screening room."

Robby said, "What about the screening room? How big's that?"

Frank said, "Regular room size. The screen's a permanent fixture, against the wall opposite the door, over where the window would be if there was a window. There's ten good-sized theater seats facing it, five on either side of a center aisle. They're in two rows, two on each side in the front row, three on each side in back. They're dark blue, with white plastic, and there's spaces between them, and ashtrays built into the left arm. They're wider than regular theater seats. And more comfortable. There's a wide space between the back row of seats and the wall of the projectionist's booth. Covered with blue carpet."

Robby said, "Wide enough for us?"

Frank said, "Guaranteed. Room to spare."

Robby said, "Any side doors into the screening room? Any other way in besides the door from the hall?"

Frank said, "No, that's it. Just the one entrance."

Robby said, "They got to have a fire exit. You can't run a theater with only one way out."

Frank said, "This isn't a theater, it's a screening room. The most people they're set up for is ten. They don't need a lot of exits."

Kelly said, "Besides, this isn't New York City."

Frank said, "I got a question of my own."

Kelly said, "Ask it."

Frank said, "What if she's got a guest?"

Kelly said, "Like who?"

Frank said, "How do I know? Somebody she meets on the way into the hotel, some old friend. Or maybe the hotel manager, he wants to be alone in a dark room with Sassi Manoon."

Kelly said, "She'll turn him down. Starnap says so."

Frank said, "What does Starnap say about chance encounters? She runs into an ex-husband on her way through the lobby. What about that?"

Kelly said, "Starnap says that if chance enters into it, altering the pattern, and it is early enough to extricate ourselves without having alerted her to our plans, we should return to the boat for further instructions. If it's too late, we've already tipped our hand, we should try to ad-lib past the interference, and if that's impossible, we should give it up, return to the boat, flee Jamaica, and work out another operation elsewhere. Starnap says that in its absence we are left to our own judgment about whether or not the pattern has been altered sufficiently to cause changes in plan or return for further instructions."

Robby said, "Sometimes I'm not so sure about Starnap."

Kelly said, "Why not?"

Robby said, "It thinks too complicated, that's why not.

Like, look at us. We want to kidnap Sassi Manoon, right? So what do we do? We steal a car. Then we bounce a forged check. Then we kidnap two men and steal their truck. We steal a Persian carpet. Before this is over, about the only thing we won't have done is spit on the sidewalk."

Frank said, "Don't be too sure."

Kelly said, "Starnap knows what it's doing. You can have perfect faith in it."

Robby said, "That's good news."

"Yeah," said Frank.

*

"Tell him he's driving too fast," said Sassi.

The chauffeur glanced in the rear-view mirror. "Yes, ma'am," he said, and eased down from thirty-five to thirty.

Benny said, "You're driving too fast."

"Yes, sir," said the chauffeur. He eased it back up to thirty-five.

Behind her shades, Sassi shut her eyes. She could only take simple progressions today; interweavings and multimedia implosions were out. She was the perfect example of the McLuhanesque mind, intending to do nothing but read from left to right forever. No crosscuts, no curlicues. No chauffeurs answering her when she tells Benny something to tell the chauffeur, then Benny telling the chauffeur and then the chauffeur answering him too. Only straight lines today, in every meaning of the term.

"We're here," said Benny, outside her closed lids.

"Of course we are," she said. Or maybe she just thought

it and didn't have the strength to say it. In any case, she didn't have the strength to open her eyes and look. What did she care where here was? *I am, therefore I am here.* Sum, ergo something or other.

The Rolls stopped. Sassi half-opened her eyes, and looked through trembling lids at a sun-dappled colored bellboy in a green jacket, reaching to open the car door. Watching the bellboy, she said, "If you'll take the dogs, Benny, I won't bitch at you for a week." Kama and Sutra, standing now, were stretching all over the place.

"Sure," Benny said.

She couldn't tell what he meant by that, and she didn't want any of those things either. Cryptic, enigmatic, all that stuff. Out with it. Hangovers require simple declarative sentences that make simple declarations.

The door swung open, and a puff of external heat entered the air-conditioned interior of the car and curled like a boa around Sassi's shins. Sassi sighed. Past the bellboy she could see the smiling faces of a welcoming committee.

"This movie better be worth it," she said.

*

"What time is it?" Kelly said.

Frank looked at his watch. "Twenty to eleven," he said. He was leaning against the left front corner of the VW. The VW and the Cortina were parked on the left verge of route A1, near Rose Hall. Across the road lay the sea, blue and calm. Kelly and Frank and Robby were clustered between the two vehicles, Frank leaning on the VW, Robby sitting on the Cortina trunk, Kelly pacing back and forth between them. All three were smoking, Kelly with the most obvious nervousness, and though Kelly had a watch of his own he'd been asking Frank the time every minute or two.

Now he snapped his cigarette away. "Time to get moving," he said.

Robby said, "Maybe we should wait five more minutes. To be on the safe side."

"According to Starnap," Kelly said, "Sassi Manoon and B. B. Bernard will quarrel within ten minutes of the beginning of the movie, and Bernard will go outside with the dogs. If it's twenty to eleven, he's out there now."

"If they got there on time," said Frank.

"Starnap says—"

"Yeah, yeah," said Frank. He shifted his weight away from the VW. "Starnap says, I know."

"Starnap doesn't make mistakes," Kelly said dangerously, daring somebody to disagree.

"Come on, Robby," Frank said.

"Okay," said Robby. He slid off the Cortina trunk.

Kelly looked at the two of them. "Starnap does know," he said.

"Nobody's arguing with you, Kelly," said Frank.

"We're doing it, aren't we?" said Robby.

"All right," said Kelly grumpily.

"It's just nerves," Robby said. "We're all nervous, that's all. There's no need to fight among ourselves."

"All right," said Kelly, still grumpy but trying not to be. "You two come along in three minutes. Right?"

"Right," said Frank.

"See you," said Robby.

Kelly waved a hand, jerkily, and walked up to get behind

the wheel of the Cortina. "Shift with the left hand," he whispered to himself. "Shift with the left hand." He could see the other two in the rear-view mirror, watching him with anticipatory grins on their faces. "Shift with the left hand," he whispered.

He started the engine, shifted with his left hand, felt great relief, and drove triumphantly out onto the highway, speeding toward Mahoe Bay Hotel in the right lane. He didn't move over till he looked out and saw a hundred-ton mile-wide maroon bus with lots of windows thundering toward him in the same lane. "Drive on the left," he told himself as the bus whistled by. "*Drive* on the left. Shift left, *drive* left. Shift left, *drive* left."

*

Kelly saw B. B. Bernard and the two Afghans mousing around some shrubbery to one side of the hotel as he drove the Cortina into the parking lot. Good. So far, everything according to plan. He left the car—gratefully—and got his clipboard from the back seat. Starnap maintained that a man with a clipboard is never questioned, because a clipboard is a sure demonstration of official status. A man with a clipboard *must* be authorized.

Kelly carried his clipboard into the hotel, and followed Frank's directions up to the second floor and down the hall to 27A, the entry to the projectionist's booth. He tried the knob there, but the door was locked.

Had there been a change of plan? He knocked on the door, waited, knocked again, waited again, and was just about to knock again when the door opened and an angry brown face said, "What? We're busy in here."

We? The projectionist was supposed to be alone. Well, it didn't matter. Kelly plunged ahead, saying, "I have to come in for a minute. This won't take long."

The projectionist looked at the clipboard, accepted it as proof of identity just the way Starnap had said he would, and grousingly said, "Well, if you got to." He stepped back and Kelly went up the high step and in, shutting the door behind him.

The room was, as Frank had said, small and crowded. The huge black projection machine on the right, looking like a robot made by ants, was whining and whirring and occasionally clanking. Its brother robot on the left was quiet. The let-down table in the middle was let down, and on it were distributed various pieces of cold chicken wrapped in wax paper, two bottles of Red Stripe beer, a bottle opener, and a deck of cards. But there was no second person present. Apparently the projectionist spoke of himself in the plural, employing the editorial "we."

"I got to start the new reel in just a minute," the projectionist said.

"I'll wait," Kelly told him.

"Good. Hold on now, I got to get by you."

It was a tight squeeze. Kelly held his clipboard over his head while the projectionist slid by him and went to man the quiet robot on the left. There was a small eyehole next to the projector's opening in the wall, and the projectionist bent to this eyehole while keeping one hand on the projector's controls.

The peephole above the table was open, too, and was

about four inches square. Leaning over the table, Kelly could see the screening room, could see the lone figure sitting in there in the dark, rear row, aisle seat. On the screen, a limping wolf crossed an icy river at night. The film flickered slightly, sometimes darker, sometimes a bit lighter, as though God hadn't known exactly how dark He wanted things that night. A massed chorus of male and female voices belted out a triumphant paean in a foreign language in the background. An off-camera voice spoke at length in perhaps the same foreign language, and white typewriter letters appeared on the screen, down near the bottom of the picture:

Vavlov was growing tired

"There!" said the projectionist, and the left-hand robot began to click and whirr. "Got to get by," he said, and crowded past Kelly again to service the right-hand robot. Kelly watched him shut it down, open it up, remove a reel of film from its innards, move an empty reel from here to there, get another reel from a case under the table and put it in place, thread the film on a route through the projector more complex than the Los Angeles Freeway system, shut the projector up again, turn to Kelly, brush his hands, and say, "Done! We've about twenty-five minutes."

"I'm sure it won't take that long," Kelly said. He hoped it wouldn't anyway. Getting his clipboard and pen into position, he said, "Your name?"

"Gillies," said the projectionist. "W. Clembert Gillies."

"W?"

"Wellington," the projectionist said, showing some embarrassment. "I never use it."

"I see." Kelly leaned forward and looked out the

peephole. She was still there. "Will our voices disturb anyone in there?" he asked. "Should we close this?"

"Oh, no," W. Clembert Gillies said. "They can't hear a
thing. We're soundproofed, see?" He pointed at all the little
holes in the walls and ceiling.

"But what about the peephole here?"

"She won't hear a word," he said. "Guaranteed."

"Very well." Kelly shrugged, knowing better than to
push it any more. He poised the pen over the clipboard.
"Now. How do you spell Gillies?"

*

Frank followed a spur of blacktop away from the main
entrance of the hotel and around to the side, parking just
around the corner. B. B. Bernard and the Afghans were off
to the right, involved with a palm tree.

Frank pointed. 'That door there," he said, "leads into the
corridor we want. The door to the stairs is just ahead on the
right."

Robby nodded. "Good."

"Now remember," Frank said, "if anybody asks us anything, I do the talking." Switching to Jamaican accent, he
said, "All I know, I got to deliver this rug."

"I suppose you think that's funny," Robby said.

Frank looked at him. "What is?"

"That you can do a native better than I can. That wig
looks rotten on you."

"It does not. I look like Laurence Olivier in *Othello.*"

"That's what I said," said Robby.

"You're just jealous," said Frank.

"No," said Robby. "It's nerves, like I told Kelly. How come you aren't doing your voices any more?"

"I don't feel like it right now," said Frank. "Come on, let's get going."

They got out of the VW, walked around to the back, opened the rear doors, and got the rug. It was rolled around a long bamboo pole, which stuck out a foot or more at each end, giving them something to grab it by.

"Heavy," said Robby.

"Wait'll we bring it back down," said Frank.

Leaving the VW rear doors open, they carried the rug into the hotel.

*

Kelly leaned forward. She was still there. What was taking them so long? He turned back to W. Clembert Gillies. "You live in Anchovy," he said.

"That's right."

"No street address?"

"No, just in Anchovy. Right in town."

"Very well." Kelly made marks on the clipboard while he hunted around for more questions to ask. "And how long," he finally said, "have you been in your present employment?"

*

When Frank uncapped the chloroform, Robby made a face and said, "Ugh. You'll be knocking *me* out in a minute."

Frank poured some onto the handkerchief, then capped

the bottle again and put it back in his pocket. "Lovely stuff," he said. "Wakes me right up."

"It would. You'll never get near her with that, it smells all over the place."

"Don't you worry about me," Frank told him. "You just be ready when I come back out."

"I'll be right here," Robby said.

Frank took a deep breath, let it out slowly, and said, "Well, here goes nothing." He opened the door and went into the screening room.

Robby stood beside the rug in the empty hall, looking nervously toward the stairs, and waited.

*

Four fat women shoveled rubble. A coloratura sang wordlessly on the soundtrack. One of the women rested, leaned on her shovel, and spoke in a foreign tongue to the woman beside her. Words appeared on the bottom of the screen:

Sometimes I worry about Vanya

Frank shut the door behind him with the hand not holding the chloroformed handkerchief. The smell of it seemed stronger here in the dark. He waited a few seconds till his eyes began to get accustomed to the darkness, till he could just make out the dark figure of the room's only occupant in the seat to the right of the aisle, rear row. Then, using Kirk Douglas' voice, he said, loudly and heartily, "Sassi! They told me you were here!" Walking swiftly forward, talking fast and loud to cover his intentions, he said, "I just flew in this morning, going to be at the dinner tonight, couldn't wait to come see you, had to say—"

He bent over her, as though to give her the standard greeting peck on the cheek, and instead clapped the handkerchief over her nose and mouth.

She struggled violently, but Frank held on for dear life, pinning her to the chair from behind, and at last her struggles lessened, eased, slowed, came to a stop. Her arms dropped to her sides, and when he released her, her head lolled.

He looked up, and the peephole in the projectionist's booth was open. Kelly was supposed to have gotten that thing shut by now. Inside there he could just see the top of Kelly's head.

Well, if Kelly kept the projectionist distracted, it wouldn't matter. Frank hurried back to the door, opened it, and left it open when he went out to the hall. "Ready," he said to Robby, half-whispering.

"Good." Robby was half-whispering, too.

They carried the rug into the screening room, set it on the floor behind the seats, and Frank shut the door.

"Hey!" Robby whispered. "I can't see a thing! Leave it open."

"And have somebody come in here? Work by feel."

There was a faint dim light reflecting back from the screen, where tanks were now rumbling through what looked like a destroyed slum. There was no music at all, nothing but a lot of squeaking tank treads.

Working mostly by feel, Robby and Frank unrolled the carpet about halfway, then picked up the body and carried it over to the rug. "Heavy," Robby gasped.

"Dead weight," Frank explained. "Unconscious people always weigh more."

(99)

"That doesn't make any sense," Robby whispered.

They put the unconscious body onto the rug and rolled the rug around her, then refastened the ropes. "Okay at this end," Frank whispered.

"Here, too," Robby whispered.

They picked up the rug again, staggering a little from the double weight, and headed out of the room, Frank opening the door when he reached it, Robby closing it again on the way by. They walked with the nonchalant boldness of honest men.

On the screen, an extreme close-up showed the seamed, lined, weary, agonized face of an old peasant woman wearing a black shawl around her head. She was talking, at length, through her tears, directly at the audience of empty seats. At the bottom of the screen it said:

Goodbye

*

"My youngest boy is six, going on seven."

Kelly glanced out the peephole. The room was empty. About time. "Fine," he said, and studied his clipboard with a critical eye. "Well, I guess that about does it," he said. "Thank you for your time."

"It's okay," said the projectionist.

Kelly left the booth, walked down the hall, down the stairs, out of the hotel, and over to the parking lot. B. B. Bernard was still mousing around with the dogs, looking at his watch and glumly smoking cigarettes.

As he was getting into the Cortina, Kelly saw the VW go by, and read the inscription on the side: MONTEGO BAY

CARPET AND UPHOLSTERY COMPANY LTD. *Fort Street, Montego Bay.* He was too far away to read the expressions on the faces of the two in the cab, but he was sure they were smiling in triumph.

Kelly got behind the wheel of the Cortina. "Shift left," he told himself, *"and* drive left. Shift left, *and* drive left."

He started the car, did everything slowly but right, and drove the Cortina out of the parking lot and down the road toward the highway. He saw the VW turn right at the highway, and a minute later he made the same turn himself.

He felt good. Starnap had worked everything out, everything, down to the smallest detail, with the kind of precision and attention to minutiae that only a machine could give to the task. And the precision had paid off. Eight hundred fifty thousand dollars' worth.

Kelly caught up with the carpet company truck before they reached the city, and drove along behind it, reading the company name on the rear doors, thinking of the value of what actually lay within those doors.

They followed A1 after it became Kent Avenue and swept out along the shore between the sea and the airport, then curved to the left, became Gloucester Avenue, and entered the in-town hotel section.

The yacht club was on the right. They parked the two vehicles near one another, but Kelly gave no sign of knowing the other two when he passed them on the street, Kelly heading for the yacht club and they going around to the rear of the VW.

Kelly went through the yacht club building and out the dock to *Nothing Ventured IV.* He noticed that Major ffork-Linton's boat was gone. Maybe the film festival had been too boisterous for the old boy after all. Or more likely for his lady.

Kelly went aboard *Nothing Ventured IV* and heard somebody tapping S-O-S-S-O etc., somewhere close by. It took him a few seconds to remember the girl, then he just shook his head. If she wanted to expend energy that way, it was all right with him.

There was a clatter up on deck, and Frank's voice called, "Help us get her down there!"

"Coming."

Kelly went back on deck, and there was the rug. Frank and Robby were panting and gasping and leaning on things. "We'll have to get it out of sight fast," Kelly said.

"Lend a hand," Frank said.

"Right." Lifting one end while the other two both lifted the other, Kelly said, "We'll have to move the truck as soon as we have her locked away with the other one. We'll leave it downtown. Then return the rented car, and—"

"Move it, Kelly," said Frank. "Talk later."

"Oh. Of course."

It *was* heavy. And they had to be careful how they banged her around, even though she was protected by two or three layers of rug, but they finally did get her down into the cabin, lying on the floor. Then, as Kelly went around closing the curtains over all the windows, Robby and Frank untied the ropes. They unrolled the rug, and Adelaide Rushby sat up and said, "Well! You boys are *certainly* going to hear about *this!*"

(9)

A Major Reversal

"You won't get away with this!" raged Sassi, tossing her proud blond mane.

The major twirled his mustache.

(10)

Coming to Terms

Frank said, "This caper's getting too crowded."

"This *room's* getting too crowded," Robby told him.

They were in the main cabin of *Nothing Ventured IV.* Jigger and Miss Rushby were sitting side by side on the sofa, both looking angry and aloof. Frank was leaning against the ladder, his pistol held negligently in his hand. Robby was walking back and forth, smoking nervously, leaving trails of smoke behind him like a tugboat. They could all hear Starnap in the other room, humming away, talking to Kelly.

"All I say," Miss Rushby said, "is you had better let us go at once, this young lady and myself, before you get into even worse trouble."

"You're damn right," said Jigger.

"Yeah, yeah," said Frank, and Kelly came back into the room.

Kelly looked grim, but not depressed. He said, "Starnap worked it out."

"Good for Starnap," said Frank, who was depressed but not grim.

Kelly said, "The Major kidnapped Sassi."

Everybody said, "What?" or "No!" or "Nonsense."

"Starnap is never wrong," Kelly said.

Robby said, "What else did Starnap say?"

"We can still work things out," Kelly told him. "Starnap says all is not lost."

"You young people," Miss Rushby said, "are completely out of your minds. The idea!"

"The idea," said Kelly, "is, the Major and this lady walked into that screening room the second B. B. Bernard took the dogs away. The Major told Sassi some lie and got her out of there. Miss Rushby sat in her place to fool the projectionist into thinking Sassi was still there. Then Miss Rushby would have walked out of the screening room just before the movie ended, and that would have been that."

"Incredible fantasy," opined Miss Rushby.

"The Major brought Sassi back here," Kelly went on, "put her on his boat, and took off."

"So we're out," Frank said.

Kelly shook his head. "No. It's more complicated now, but we can still work it."

Miss Rushby said to Jigger, "Do you know these young men, my dear?"

"No," said Jigger. "They kidnapped *me* last night. They got kidnapping on the brain."

"They will come," Miss Rushby said, "to no good end."

"The sooner the better," said Jigger.

Robby said, "How do we work it, Kelly? We don't have

Sassi and we don't know where she is."

"We have her," Kelly said, pointing to Miss Rushby. "She and the Major would have worked out a place to hook up together again sometime today. She won't be at the meeting place. Sooner or later he'll start looking for her, and then he'll have to come out in the open, and then we can make a deal."

Robby said, "What kind of deal?"

"We trade," Kelly said. He pointed at Miss Rushby. "Sassi for her."

"That's quite complimentary, I'm sure," said Miss Rushby. "But I assure you, young man—"

"Starnap is never wrong," Kelly told her.

"I don't know who this Starnap is—"

"Kelly's machine," Frank said.

"A computer," Robby explained. "And Kelly's right, Miss Rushby. This computer is never wrong. If it says the Major kidnapped Sassi Manoon and you stayed in her place to give him time to make a getaway, then that's what happened. There's no point denying it, because we just won't believe you."

Miss Rushby looked from face to face. "Then what will you do?"

"Keep you," Robby said gently. "Until we hear from the Major."

"Poor Alfred," she said, "will be very worried. Very worried. He won't know how to get in touch with me."

"You could save him that worry," Frank said.

Miss Rushby looked up warily. "How's that, young man?"

"Tell us where you're supposed to meet him. Then we'll all go there and talk terms."

"Watch it!" Jigger said. "You tell them anything, they'll kidnap this Major of yours, too."

"Of course, my dear," said Miss Rushby. "I am well aware of the danger."

"What about the danger to yourself, Miss Rushby?" Robby asked.

"Danger to myself?" She smiled sweetly around at the three of them. "I don't believe I'm really in that much danger," she said. "You can't hold us prisoner forever, and I really don't believe you would kill us. You just aren't the murdering type."

"Well, I'm not," Robby admitted. "And Frank wouldn't kill anybody either, you're right about that. But I don't know about Kelly. He hates to be frustrated. I don't think I'd take a chance on him myself."

Miss Rushby looked at Kelly, who glared at her with all the fury of the world's youngest mad scientist at bay. "Well," said Miss Rushby, a bit uncertain now. She dibbled at her throat lace.

"We aren't greedy," Robby said softly, pressing his advantage. "I'm sure we could work out some sort of deal with you and the Major. No one would get as much as originally planned, but everyone would get something."

"They're crazy," Jigger said, and turned to look at Miss Rushby. She frowned at the thoughtful expression on Miss Rushby's face.

Frank said, "How much were you two going to ask?"

Miss Rushby was clearly thinking hard. Finally she said, "What sort of guarantee could we have of full participation?"

Jigger said, "What?"

"You and the Major can take care of yourselves," Frank said. "We'll let the Major keep Sassi and we'll keep you. When the ransom's picked up—"

Jigger said, "What *is* this?"

"Quiet, girl," said Miss Rushby. To Frank she said, "Yes? Go on."

"When the ransom's picked up," Frank said, "we'll divvy it up, you go back to the Major, Sassi goes home, and everybody's happy."

Jigger said, "You *did* do it!"

"Hush, girl! Young man, I want to think about this."

Robby said, "What time are you supposed to meet the Major?"

"I said I want to think about it."

"Go ahead and think," Kelly said. "We can wait."

Miss Rushby sat back and looked pained, which apparently meant she was thinking.

Jigger looked from face to face in growing panic. "Everybody's crazy!" she shouted. "Everybody! I'm the only sane one left in the whole world!"

"Quiet," Frank told her. "The lady's thinking."

Miss Rushby said, "We'd have to have an exchange of hostages, of course. Not just me. One of you would have to stay with Alfred."

"Me," Frank said. "That's easy."

"Unarmed."

"Naturally," Frank said.

Miss Rushby sighed. "We planned to ask fifty thousand," she said.

"My *God!*" Jigger shrieked.

Kelly snapped, "Get her out of here, Robby. Lady, fifty thousand is peanuts."

"Come along," Robby said.

Jigger, wild-eyed, allowed herself to be led away.

"How much were you thinking of?" Miss Rushby asked.

"Eight hundred fifty thousand."

Frank said, "That's her salary for one movie."

"That's outlandish," Miss Rushby said. "Out of the question. No one would pay such a price."

Kelly said, "Lady, do you realize how much Sassi Manoon's pictures *make? Each?*"

"You couldn't—"

"You've got to think—"

"Sit down, Kelly," Frank said. "Let's work this out."

They began to dicker.

*

"Rule Britannia," sang the Major, "Britannia rules the waves, *tum* tum teetley tum tum tee tee tee."

Life, deemed the Major, was good. He stood here at the wheel of *Redoubtable,* moving briskly westward through a calm and lovely sea, the isle of Jamaica a green extravagance to his left, *Redoubtable's* Rolls Royce engines purring away, no other human being in sight, all lovely, all good, all beautiful. The Manoon woman had stopped hammering on the door of the aft cabin, into which he had locked her, and in just a few moments now he would be reunited with Adelaide. Tum tee *tum.*

It had gone beautifully. He'd spirited the Manoon woman away without a hitch. If all had gone equally well with Adelaide—and there was no reason it shouldn't have — then she'd left the screening room just before the finish of that dreadful film, she'd driven away in the little car they'd rented yesterday, she'd taken route A1 westward out of Montego Bay, she'd traveled some thirty-two miles, and had stopped at last on a lonely stretch of road between Lances Bay and Cousins Cove where the road skirted an empty beach and where their rowboat was hidden, and she was calmly waiting now for him to appear offshore, at which point she would row out to meet him, and they would head directly for their refuge. Tem ta-*rum* pum.

The Major spun the wheel. *Redoubtable* veered to the left, southward. He was near the western edge of the island now, the land slanting away from him off to the right. Lucea was several miles to the left, nothing much was to the right. And the rendezvous point ought to be . . . just about . . . *there.*

A boat?

The Major eased back on the throttle, and *Redoubtable* settled her nose a bit into the water as she slowed. Yes, there was a boat there, directly ahead of him between him and the shore, exactly where he had intended to heave to and wait for Adelaide to row out to him. A familiar boat, somehow. Familiar.

And Adelaide? There was nothing on shore. He could see the road there, a tiny slender ribbon, and there was nothing on it at all. Nothing on the beach, no one anywhere.

A figure was waving to him from the other boat. It looked like—

—Adelaide.

And now he recognized the boat, knew it for the one owned by that trio of pointless young men. What on earth were they doing here, and why on earth was Adelaide with them?

With a premonition that stilled the song on his lips, Major ffork-Linton steered toward the other vessel.

*

"Care for a drink?" asked the Major, coldly polite.

"No, thank you," said Robby.

Kelly snorted. "A mickey? Let's get to business."

"I assure you," said the Major, but let it go at that.

The three were aboard *Redoubtable* for the confab. Sassi Manoon was locked away in another part of *Redoubtable.* Jigger and Miss Rushby were locked away aboard *Nothing Ventured IV,* with Frank on guard.

"We're empowered to speak for our other partner," Kelly now told the Major, "and Miss Rushby tells us you're empowered to speak for her."

The Major nodded. "Of course. Won't you at least sit down? I promise the chairs are not booby-trapped."

"Thank you," said Robby.

They all took seats, and the Major said, "Now. Frankly, I'm at a loss. What is my friend doing on your boat? What are you all doing in this deserted place?"

"You broke into our caper," Kelly told him. "It worked like a charm, just the way it was supposed to, and we wound up with Miss Rushby."

"I beg your pardon. Did you say *I* broke into *your* caper?"

Robby explained, "We were after Sassi, too."

The Major frowned. "Sassi? I don't quite understand."

"The kidnapping," Robby said.

(*111*)

"Kidnapping? You mean Sassi Manoon?" The Major looked at them with shocked innocence. "Surely you aren't asking me to join you in some sort of illegal—"

"Come off it, Major," said Kelly. "We've had a long talk with your partner. We stole her by mistake out of that screening room."

"You—" The Major stared from face to face, then suddenly burst out, "You were doing it, too!"

"Of course. That's what we've been saying."

"Oh, ho ho," said the Major. He began boisterously to laugh, going, "Ho ho ho ho." His face was getting red. He held his sides and laughed: "Ho ho ho."

They waited till he'd subsided, and then Kelly said, "So you broke into our caper."

"Oh, no, young man," said the Major, wiping his eyes with his handkerchief. "You broke into *my* caper, if it comes to that."

"Which is which doesn't matter," Robby said. "The point is, we're all in it together now."

"I hardly see how you can draw that conclusion," the Major said. "I have Miss Manoon."

Kelly said, "We have Miss Rushby."

The Major looked startled, then said, "I see."

"So we work together," Kelly said.

"Unless you'd like to trade even," Robby suggested. "If you don't want to work with us, that is."

"And leave with nothing?"

"With Miss Rushby," Robby pointed out.

The Major shook his head. "What is your other proposition?"

Kelly said, "Miss Rushby told us you were figuring on asking fifty thousand."

The Major pursed his lips and said, "You *have* been chatting with her, haven't you?"

"That was too little," Kelly told him. "She's worth millions."

"You couldn't get millions," the Major said gently.

"I know it. What we were going to ask was her salary for one movie. Eight hundred fifty thousand dollars."

The Major made a face. "My dear boy, that's unthinkable!"

"Miss Rushby convinced Starnap that was too much to ask," Kelly admitted. "So we worked out a compromise figure. Four hundred thousand."

"Four—"

"It's high, but we'll get it. And that makes one hundred thousand for each of us, and one hundred thousand for you and Miss Rushby together."

Robby said, "This way, you'll get twice as much as you figured."

"And it's safer," Kelly added. "We've got a better way worked out for getting the ransom. That Swiss bank of yours wouldn't touch the deposit if they knew it was ransom."

Robby said, "But you've got a better hideout than we'd figured on. We were just going to lie low in a cove around on the western side of the island till after the ransom was paid."

"You'd have been picked up in no time," the Major told him.

"You may be right," Robby said.

"Not necessarily," said Kelly. "Starnap said it would work if we were careful. It said it was the best we could do."

"I take it," said the Major, "you want me to lead you to the place I had in mind for myself."

"Yes," said Robby. "The island."

"And I'm supposed to trust you to keep me on as a full partner after we get there."

"Of course not," Kelly snapped. "Nobody trusts anybody."

The Major made a wintry smile.

Robby said, "We have Miss Rushby, to make sure you won't try anything. You have Sassi, and we'll give you Frank."

"Unarmed," said Kelly.

"We aren't killers," said Robby. "And I don't think you and Miss Rushby are either. Short of murder, there's nothing any of us can do to get free of any of the others before this thing is over."

"We know too much about each other," said Kelly. "We could all pay back a double-cross with interest."

"That's perfectly true," said the Major. He sighed, drilled his fingertips on his chair arm, pursed his lips, gazed out the window toward the other boat, shrugged, and finally said, "Very well. I can see where my best interests lie."

"Good," said Kelly.

"But since we are stuck with one another in any event, why bother with hostages? Why not return Miss Rushby, and keep your friend?"

"When we get to the island," Robby said.

"With Frank over here and Miss Rushby with us," Kelly said, "nobody's likely to try any run-out powder."

"Run-out powder?" The Major grimaced. "I suppose I understand that. Very well." He got to his feet. "We would appear," he said, "to be partners."

"That's good," said Robby. He and Kelly also rose.

"But," said the Major, speaking to Kelly, "it doesn't seem the handshake sort of partnership, does it?"

"No," said Kelly. "We'll send Frank right over to you," he said, "and then we'll follow you to your island."

"Very well."

The Major watched them go over the side into their dinghy and row back toward *Nothing Ventured IV.* There on deck was the third young man, watching.

The Creswel boy had been right about one thing; none of them was a killer. If only he *were* a killer, the Major thought, he could take his Walther out right now and pot all three of them, the two in the dinghy and the one on the other boat over there.

"Drat," said the Major.

(*11*)

Afloat

Sassi prowled her pigmy prison like a provoked panther. When it had finally become evident that battering at the door wasn't going to do her any good, nor was shouting, nor was kicking the wall, nor was throwing the pillows around and dumping the contents of the drawers on the floor, she'd sat down on the bed to sulk and lick her knuckles. But when the boat had stopped, she'd found her own inaction no longer supportable, and so she'd gotten up and had started to march.

Some march. Three strides and about-face Three strides and about-face. This cabin wasn't meant for promenades.

What was happening out there? All she could see from the portholes was water and sky. Listening at the door she could hear voices, but not what they were saying. Then she couldn't even hear voices.

What was going on? Ever since that limey bastard had walked into the screening room and told her Kama had been run over by a tourist, she'd been in a state, first of panic, then—when he'd flashed that nasty gun of his and forced her into his automobile—of terror, then—when he'd gagged her and tied her to a chair on the boat here—of outrage, and most recently—when he'd switched her from the chair to this room—of bewilderment. What was happening? What did he want from her? Not the fate worse than death, he was hardly the type. A kidnapping? That was ridiculous!

The door opened and a young guy walked in, smiling. "Hello, there," he said. The door shut again behind him, and Sassi heard the lock being refastened.

"I've been in this picture," she said. "You're here to rescue me."

"Not exactly," said the young guy, still smiling. "I'm one of the kidnappers." He walked over and looked out the porthole. "We won't be stuck together long," he said.

Sassi felt the boat getting into motion again. She said, in a dazed sort of way, "You're one of the kidnappers?"

"That's right. It's sort of complicated. Right now I'm a prisoner too, but when we get to the island we'll—"

"How come you sound like Michael Caine?"

His smile turned more boyish and his voice turned James Stewart. "Well, gosh, ma'am, I couldn't, I couldn't just *say*."

"Oh, my God," cried Sassi, "it does imitations. There *is* a fate worse than death!"

*

Robby sat in one of the two fixed chairs on the top deck, watching the Major's boat surge through the blue sea ahead, leaving an endless running white *V* into which *Nothing Ventured IV* endlessly chased. The two sparkling boats on the sparkling sea beneath the sparkling sky in the sparkling sunlight made a beautiful sight, but Robby was in no mood for beauty. Robby was being glum.

There were too many complications. Too many people involved, too many chances for things to go wrong. Instead of three kidnappers, there were now five, and instead of one kidnappee, there were now two. There was less money to be made, there were more risks, and all in all Robby didn't like it a damn bit. But what else was there to do? Circumstances had conspired against them.

He was distracted from his gloomy thoughts by a noise behind him. Looking around, he saw Miss Rushby coming up the steps, very Victorian and out of place. "May I join you?" she asked, and paused at the head of the steps to catch her breath.

Robby gestured at the other chair. "Please do."

"Thank you." She settled herself with a great flurry of contented sighs and skirt adjustments, then shook her head and said, "What a blessing it is to be away from that girl. Do you know, she refuses to believe I won't plot some sort of escape with her?"

"It's hard to tell who's on whose side sometimes," Robby said.

"That is true. How does she happen to be here at all?"

Robby had been needing some sort of distraction from his somber thoughts, and Miss Rushby for some reason had a restful effect on the people in her presence. Robby found

(118)

himself telling her all about last night, about the activities at the party, and Jigger's stumbling across Kelly, and then the capture of Jigger and the return of Kelly, and at the end of it all Miss Rushby shook her head sympathetically and said, "My. You three seem to have had a much harder time of it than Alfred and myself."

"You don't seem right for something like this," Robby told her, "if you don't mind my saying so. You and the Major."

"Oh, don't I know it," Miss Rushby said ruefully. "We thought and thought before deciding to go ahead with it. But we did need a great deal of money quickly, and at last this seemed the only way to get it."

"All of a sudden you needed money?" Robby couldn't picture it.

"For our boy Percy."

"Your boy?"

Miss Rushby laughed in an embarrassed way and said, "Oh, the Major and I are married, we've been husband and wife thirty-seven years next April."

"But—"

"You mean my name?" Miss Rushby smiled her sweet smile and leaned forward confidentially, saying, "That isn't my real name. Nor is the Major using his own name."

"But—" Robby was at a loss. "I thought you knew people in England. That Spence guy was supposed to be the son of an old friend."

"Well, of course," Miss Rushby said. "We are very well known under these names. When Alfred and I arrived in the United States thirty-four years ago we were sure of two things. First, because of the Depression—that was why we'd left England—we were going to have to make our way by our wits, which meant we daren't travel under our own names. Family, you know."

"Yes," said Robby in a dazed sort of way.

"And second," Miss Rushby said, "we knew we would be much likelier to succeed if we were believed both to be single. And a bit racy."

"You've lived under fake names for thirty-four years."

Miss Rushby nodded. "Yes, we have. But that's all coming to an end. After this adventure, Alfred and I intend to retire. I hope you'll understand if I don't tell you where, but in our retirement we shall return to our rightful names and admit to being husband and wife."

Robby looked at the Major's boat, out there ahead of them, then back at Miss Rushby. "You're a couple of con artists," he said.

"I have never been partial to American slang, I must admit," Miss Rushby said, "no matter how long I have been exposed to it. But I suppose the phrase is accurate. Once the contract-bridge craze of the thirties died down, it did become necessary for us to branch out into other endeavors, but I assure you this is absolutely the first and last affair of *this* sort we have ever been involved in."

"Us, too," said Robby. "We want to make a quick killing and retire."

Miss Rushby looked at him. "Retire? At your age? From what?"

Robby shrugged. "From the rat race," he said. "How come your son needs money all of a sudden?"

"Poor Percy," Miss Rushby said, and shook her head with long-suffering maternal compassion. "He will try to follow in our footsteps, so to speak, his father's and mine, and things always will go wrong for him. Nothing really serious, just embarrassments and minor difficulties, until this last time, but apparently he will never learn."

"What's his problem now?"

"Have you ever heard of Undurwa?"

Robby shook his head.

"It's one of the new African countries," Miss Rushby said. "Or perhaps it *was* one of them, or wants to be one of them, or is seceding from one of them, I never did get it straight. Those natives there have no more idea of self-government than—oh, I am sorry." And she blushed beet-red.

"I was born in Boston," Robby said.

Miss Rushby seemed a little confused by that. "Yes," she said, "but still—"

Robby sighed. "Tell me," he said, "about Percy and this whatever-it-is in Africa."

"Undurwa."

"Underwear, that's it."

"Yes," said Miss Rushby. "Well, it seems Percy sold some rifles and ammunition to a colonel in the southwestern province. I do remember that, it was the southwestern province."

"Weren't the rifles any good?"

"They didn't exist," Miss Rushby said. "And poor Percy didn't leave the country fast enough. So now they're holding him, and the colonel wants his money back, and Percy has one month to get it for him."

"Where's the money he got from the colonel?"

"He sent it out of the country with a young lady he met last year in Mozambique. She hasn't been heard from where he was supposed to meet her."

"Oh," said Robby.

(*121*)

"Yes," said Miss Rushby. "Percy is too awfully trusting sometimes, I can't think which side of the family he got it from."

"How much?" Robby asked.

"Twenty-one thousand dollars. We planned to use the rest for our retirement." Miss Rushby leaned forward again, saying, "You do understand now why we chose this method, don't you? We couldn't very well rob a bank or anything of a violent nature like that, we just aren't of a sort to bring that kind of thing off. And our normal methods, though they have kept us solvent over the years, are hardly useful for raising a lot of cash in a hurry. Also, Percy has been kidnapped, in a way, and is being held for ransom, so we decided to fight fire with fire."

"It's too bad we were both reaching for the same match," said Robby. "How long before we reach this island of the Major's?"

Miss Rushby looked out to sea, then said, "Oh, it shouldn't be long now. It's really quite lovely, too, and on a clear day like this sometimes you can actually see Cuba, miles and miles away."

"The reason I asked," Robby said, "is they've got to know Sassi's gone by now."

"Hours ago, I should think."

"They might decide," Robby said, "to use helicopters."

Miss Rushby gave a quick apprehensive look at the empty sky, then laughed and said, "Oh, no. Not this soon."

"Why not?"

"In the first place," she said, "there has never till now been a kidnapping on the island of Jamaica. Isn't that interesting? Kidnapping is almost exclusively an American idea. Kidnapping for ransom, I mean."

"What about during the Crusades? Knights were always being held for ransom."

"That's perfectly true," said Miss Rushby, "but in the twentieth century the practice is almost entirely American. So the local authorities won't really be equipped to handle it. And the first outside authorities they'll bring in will be British, who won't know that much more than they. They'll search around Montego Bay for a while, then look in other areas of the island, and then at last they'll think of the sea."

"If I lived on an island," Robby said, "the first place I'd think of would be the sea."

"I know a number of New Yorkers," Miss Rushby said, "and they live on an island, but they *never* think of the sea."

"That isn't the same thing," Robby said.

"They won't think of the sea at all today," Miss Rushby said. "I'm convinced of it. But in any event we'll be at the island very soon now and safely out of sight."

"Don't people ever stop on this island?"

"Oh, no, not at all. It's privately owned, and the fishermen know they aren't permitted to land. But we happen to know the owners are in Switzerland right now and won't be back in this part of the world for another three months. We were their house guests a few years ago. But the place is absolutely deserted now."

"It won't be for long," Robby said.

*

The cabin door opened and the Major put his head in to say, "We're here."

"Good," said Frank. He'd found his first taste of prison less than promising.

The Major nodded and went away, leaving the door open. Frank turned to Sassi Manoon, sitting on the bed over there with her legs crossed, a cigarette dangling from one hand. He said, "You coming?"

She looked at him. "Is that supposed to be funny?"

"What? Oh, yeah, I see. Come on along."

It was the first time Frank had ever been this close to a sex symbol, and he was finding the experience strangely like novocaine. He knew she was there, he knew she had to be having some sort of effect on his nerves, but he couldn't feel a thing.

He'd been pondering that, during their long silent imprisonment together, and he'd finally decided it was because she wasn't real. Oh, she was *real* enough in the ordinary sense, she was flesh and blood and all that, but between the fact of her and his perception of her there hung a mist of fantasy, a veil of make-believe, in Technicolor and widescreen. He couldn't get himself to think of her as constructed of anything but plastic, and it was hard to get horny over plastic.

Now, as he was about to leave the cabin and follow the Major up on deck, he was surprised to see her hanging back a little, a pale look around her eyes. He said, "What's the matter?"

"What happens?" she said. "What happens now?"

"We're at the island," Frank said.

"What *happens?*" she said.

He couldn't believe she was afraid. Plastic has no fears. He said, "Nothing happens. We keep you till they pay the ransom, then we let you go."

"That's all?"

She *was* afraid. Frank moved toward her, meaning to be reassuring, and was startled when she backed away from him. He stopped where he was. "That's all," he said. "Honest, lady. You won't get hurt or anything."

He watched her getting a grip on herself. How could he have known it was a false face when he'd first come in here and she'd been so snappy and self-assured? Or maybe it was real then, but the silent traveling since had worn down her confidence. Anyway, right now she wasn't a plastic make-believe doll at all, she was a nervous worried person. And he was partially responsible.

Frank didn't like that, it embarrassed him and made him penitent. He never wanted to cause anybody unease. "Look," he said, wanting to make amends, "it won't be so bad. You'll just lie around and rest a couple days, that's all. And there's two other women here to keep you company. It won't be bad."

She smiled, and the expression was a very complex thing. In it he could read relief and irony and appreciation and cynicism and reality and façade all combined together, no attitude yet having control of the situation. "Okay," she said. "Let's go see the accommodations."

"Right this way," he said, smiling back, motioning for her to precede him, making a cheerful joke out of it, pleased that he'd made her feel better. She went first, and going up the steep steps behind her he at last did become aware of the fact that she was real. Very real.

"Um," said Frank.

PART TWO

PEOPLE

(1)

To the Manor Borne

Kelly finished his tour of the manor on a third-floor balcony. The sun, far away across the endless violet water, was just settling below the horizon. The sky was too beautiful to be anything but a creation of Walt Disney Studios, and in its light the tiny island was ornately green and darkly luxurious.

It was a good island, really, ideal for its present use. A tiny green button on the blue vest of the Caribbean, it was mostly jungle, with only this one cleared area around the manor on the eastern shore. The only building on the island, the manor was three stories high and widely rambling, with twenty-three rooms and seven baths. Porches, patios, terraces, and balconies afforded panoramic views in all directions. The furniture tended heavily to wicker and

bamboo, but some of the bedrooms were elaborately ap-
pointed and the basements were fully supplied with
canned foods and excellent wines. The two bars were kept
well-stocked, the ham radio set on the top floor was in fine
working order, and the cove in front featured a magnificent
crescent-shaped white sand beach. Just the place for a hideout.

The only lack was a dock, which was why the boats were
now anchored in the cove; they'd come ashore in the
dinghys. But it was a minor omission, compared to the assets
of the place.

Kelly had delayed touring the house until his work of the
day was done. To complete the first phase of the caper he
had still to inform the authorities of the amount and disposition of the ransom, and that's what he'd done as soon as
they'd come ashore. While the ham equipment had
warmed up he and the Major had used the old L.C. Smith
typewriter in the radio room to prepare their message, so
they would be sure to present it clearly when they got
themselves a listener. Then Kelly had sat at the mike, re-
peating, "CQ, CQ, CQ," until at last they'd roused a pharmacist in San Juan, who had come on expecting the sort of
chat about tubes and frequencies that ham radio operators
never tire of, and who had refused to believe for the longest
time that Kelly wasn't pulling his leg. But when finally he
had accepted the thought that Kelly was serious, he said,
"Is it okay if I tape what you say? I wouldn't want to get
it wrong."

Ham radio equipment was notoriously bad at accurate
reproduction of voices, so Kelly said fine and then read the
prepared statement into the mike:

"Sassi Manoon is alive and well. If she is to be returned,

a ransom of four hundred thousand dollars must be paid. This money, in unmarked United States currency, must be sealed in a watertight container and dropped with a yellow marked buoy in the sea at latitude nineteen degrees twelve minutes north and longitude seventy-eight degrees five minutes west. It must be dropped at precisely four P.M. on Monday, December 4th. No ships or planes are to be in the area. If the money is not delivered, or if it is marked or watched, Sassi Manoon will never be seen alive again. This is the only message we will make, as we do not want the authorities to trace us through triangulation of later broadcasts. We are not listening to the radio or reading newspapers, and so can receive no messages other than the delivery of the money at the proper time. We do not wish to harm Miss Manoon, and promise her safe return if the money is paid."

The pharmacist had wanted to talk when Kelly was done, but Kelly had merely told him to report to the authorities and had then signed off. Now there was nothing to do but wait till Monday afternoon and see what happened. In the meantime, he had taken a grand tour of the manor, had found it in many respects quite similar to what he had in mind for himself when this was all over, and had finished the tour on the third-floor west balcony, just as the sun was setting.

He found Jigger there, sourly studying the sun. Both she and Sassi were free to go wherever they wanted on the island, since there were no weapons they could get to, the radio room was locked up, neither boat would start without an ignition key, and they wouldn't get very far on the open sea in an open dinghy.

Jigger turned her head when Kelly stepped outside,

(131)

increased the sourness of her expression, and said, "You."

"That's all right," Kelly said. "I won't bother you." He went over to the edge and looked down at the pocket jungle below.

"You do bother me," she said. "You bother me all the time. I should have screamed last night when I had the chance, in Sir Albert's house. I shouldn't have taken pity on you."

The word *pity* stung. "What you shouldn't have done," Kelly answered, "was get so greedy. You wanted to know what was going on because you wanted in on it. You didn't fool me for a second."

"In on it? In on kidnapping? You must be crazy."

"We'll see," Kelly said.

"In the first place," Jigger told him, "you'll never get away with it."

"We'll see," Kelly said.

"And even if you do," Jigger said, "I could identify you. And so could Sassi. So what are you going to do, kill us?"

"No," Kelly said. "I just won't go places where you are. The police can show you rogue's gallery pictures, but I won't be there. You'll never see me again, so how can you identify me?"

"My time will come," she said darkly.

Kelly looked at her. She was really very pretty, even though her brow was furrowed by anger. Normally, of course, he would have gone somewhere else on finding another person out here, and half of him had wanted to do so this time, but the other half found itself intrigued by this girl, had been intrigued by her since he'd first semi-seen her through smashed glasses in B.B. Bernard's bedroom, and it was that half that had kept him out here on the balcony and in this conversation. It was also that half which now prompted him to say, "In a way, I'm sorry you won't see me again."

"Are you?" she said snottily. "Well, I'm not."

It was the sort of rebuff human beings always gave other human beings, and Kelly realized he shouldn't have expected anything else. Annoyed with himself for having forgotten what he knew about people, he shrugged his shoulders in irritation and left the balcony. A little kalah with Starnap was what he really wanted anyway. But going downstairs he couldn't help but regret that she hadn't turned out to be different from all the rest.

*

Sassi counted rooms, and the bar was number eleven. That was a good number to quit on, a lucky number. She found a glass, found ice, found Scotch, found sweet vermouth, and combined them in a way pleasing to eye and palate. She then sat down in a handy black leather chair, gazed at the black rectangle of night outside a handy window, and considered her situation and prospects.

They didn't seem to her entirely bad. Now that she'd had a chance to look at the gang who'd kidnapped her, she'd entirely lost her fear for her own safety. What a crew! It was the damnedest example of miscasting she'd ever seen. With the possible exception of the Major, there wasn't one of this mob who looked right for the part, and even the Major looked more slick than sinister.

Though why should they look sinister? Sassi could see

this affair now for what it actually was, and there was nothing sinister about it. It was a straightforward business proposition, that's all. They were holding her until the studio coughed up X dollars. Simple enough. She'd had agents doing the same thing for years.

So there was nothing to worry about. All she had to do was sit back and relax until the business dickering was done, and then she'd go back to work. Nothing to it.

Nothing in the glass, either. Sassi, feeling more and more at ease with the world, got up and made herself a fresh drink. She was on her way back to her chair when in came her co-kidnappee, the girl who called herself Jigger. "Welcome to Key Largo," Sassi said, and sat down again.

Jigger came over, looking tense. "I've been looking for you," she said. Her face was intent, her voice low with meaning.

"You have?"

"We've got to make plans."

Sassi frowned at her. "What plans?"

"To get out of here," Jigger said, as though it was the most obvious thing in the world.

Sassi stared at her in disbelief. "To do what?"

"Get out of here," Jigger repeated, low and urgent. "I've got some ideas, how we could do it."

"You're kidding," Sassi said.

"We could do it," Jigger insisted. "You think we couldn't outfox these guys?"

Sassi was about to tell her what she thought when she saw Jigger's expression suddenly change, becoming wary and guarded. Someone else had come in.

Twisting around, Sassi saw it was the boy with the voices, her friend from the boat. "There it is," he said, pointing at the bar. "I've been looking for that thing. Hello, ladies. May I join you?"

"Be our guest," Sassi told him. "We were just having a caucus of the escape committee."

Otto Preminger replied, "Zis Stalag is guaranteed escape-proof, I guarantee it." He went on over to the bar.

Jigger, her voice loaded with meaning, said, "I'll talk to you later, Sassi," and drifted out of the room.

"Sure," Sassi told her back. When Jigger was safely gone, Sassi got to her feet, went over to the bar where her friend was making himself a drink that seemed to be mostly ice cubes in a tall glass, and said, "Buddy, you're a life-saver."

"Frank," he said. "Call me Frank."

"Frank," Sassi said, "you saved my life."

"If we expect to get repeat business," Frank said, wiping the bar with a rag, "we got to have satisfied customers. You come in this joint often?"

"Every time I'm in the neighborhood," Sassi told him. She pushed her glass toward him. "Put a little more sweet vermouth in that, will you?"

"Ugh," he said, but he did it. Pushing the glass back, he said, "How come I saved your life?"

"Because you're good-hearted, I guess," she said. "Is there a radio around here?"

"You want to hear the news?"

There was a gleam in his eye. She pointed at him and said, "You do Walter Cronkite, I'm walking out."

The gleam faded, but then he looked reminiscent instead. "You know who I miss?" he said. "John Cameron Swayze. I could do a John Cameron Swayze to make you look for the picture, but what good is it now?"

"I'd look for the off switch," she said.

"That's the trouble with you big stars," he told her. "Jealous of the talents on the way up."

Sassi started to laugh, but then she thought, That's ridiculous. I'm swapping jokes with a guy that kidnapped me. Then she thought, What the hell, and went on laughing.

*

It was midnight, and the Major and Miss Rushby were playing gin. The Major was dealing, till Miss Rushby said, "I saw that. Seconds. You gave yourself my card."

The Major looked at the deck in his hands and shook his head. "I must be getting tired," he said. "We'll just play this hand, and then to bed."

"My card, Alfred."

The Major pushed a card from his side of the table to hers.

"Not that one," she said, pushed it back, and selected another. "This one."

He grabbed her hand. "Not that one either, and you know it."

"The deuce of diamonds," she said. "I'll swear that's the deuce of diamonds."

"Nonsense," he said. "Here's the deuce of diamonds." He flipped over a third card. Touching a fourth, he said, "This one's yours."

"Then I'm getting tired, too," she said. "Enough of cards." She pushed back from the table, got to her feet, and stretched in a restricted and ladylike way.

The Major, riffling the cards together, said, "The question is, what about these young men?"

"They do come in handy," Miss Rushby said. "Guarding

the prisoners and so on. And their ransom idea is brilliant."

"The question remains," the Major said. "What about afterward?"

"I should think," Miss Rushby said, "they'll be watching for us to do something to their boat. So perhaps we'd best do something to our own instead, and when the time comes, leave in theirs. We will have to give up *Redoubtable* in any event, after this."

"That would mean," the Major said, "getting the key from young Kelly. Not too easy, that."

"It just might be possible," Miss Rushby said. "The Jigger person is still somewhat confused about my status, and if anyone could slip the key away from Kelly it would be she. And if I were to suggest it to her, to help us escape—"

"Capital!" said the Major. "Just the ticket."

"I'll talk to her tomorrow."

"Excellent." The Major riffled the cards. "One more hand before bed?"

"Oh, Alfred," Miss Rushby said, and sat down. "But mind your dealing," she said.

(2)

Breakfast

Miss Rushby raised the meat cleaver high and brought it down with a *clop* on the chopping block. When she raised it again, the tea bag was in two sections. She discarded the section with the tag, the staple, and the empty end of bag, carefully picked up the full section and emptied it into the teapot on the counter to her left. She then took another tea bag from the package, placed it carefully on the block, and raised the meat cleaver again.

A voice said, "Wouldn't it be easier—?"

"Oh," said Miss Rushby, and jumped a foot. Dropping the cleaver on the counter, she looked around and saw Sassi Manoon standing there, just as startled as she was. She said, "My dear, don't ever come up behind a person without a sound like that."

⟋ "I'm sorry," Sassi said. "I know how that is." She looked past Miss Rushby. "I was going to say," she said, "wouldn't it be easier to do that with scissors?"

"What, this?" Miss Rushby looked at the bag on the block. "Yes, I suppose it would," she said. "But there weren't any in the utensil drawer. And besides, I do detest these little bandages so." She picked up the cleaver again. "Not that the tea inside them is worth the effort," she said, and decapitated another tea bag.

Sassi said, "Is there anything I can do? You're making breakfast, aren't you?"

"What there is," Miss Rushby said. "No eggs, I'm afraid. But there was some bacon in the freezer downstairs, I have a package thawing in that warm water there. And we have powdered everything. Powdered coffee, powdered milk, powdered hotcake mix."

"The way I see it," Sassi said, "we add water to the powdered milk, then add that to the powdered hotcake mix. We add water to the powdered coffee, then we combine the watered powdered coffee and the watered powdered milk. Too bad we don't have powdered sugar."

"We have," Miss Rushby said, pointing at a cabinet. "Confectioners'."

"Never mind," Sassi said, and Kelly came in. Sassi said to him, "You want pancakes?"

"Hotcakes," said Miss Rushby.

"Flapjacks," Kelly said. "But all I want is coffee."

"There's powdered," Miss Rushby said.

"Instant," said Kelly. "Do you need a match with this stove?"

"Yes," Miss Rushby said, a trifle stiffly. She didn't like

(*1 3 9*)

having all her words rejected like that.

Alfred came in, then, smoothing his mustache. "Morning, Adelaide," he said. "Lovely day. Lovely."

"Good morning," said Miss Rushby. "Yes, it is."

"Sea air," Alfred announced. "Nothing like it to give one an appetite."

"I'm making pancakes," Sassi told him.

He looked pleased. "You mean hotcakes?"

"She means flapjacks," Kelly said.

"Six for me," Alfred said, unperturbed.

For a while nothing further was said. Miss Rushby finished slaughtering tea bags and put the water on to boil. Kelly was making coffee. Sassi was making pancakes and had dragooned Alfred into making milk.

Miss Rushby had been hoping to talk to Jigger before breakfast, but obviously that was not to be. Oh, well, afterward would serve. At the moment the kitchen was steadily filling up. Frank came in next, and Miss Rushby set him to setting the table.

Robby came in a few minutes after Frank. He sniffed the air and said, "Ah! Wheatcakes!"

"Flapjacks," said Kelly.

"Hotcakes," said Miss Rushby.

"Pancakes," said Sassi.

"I believe Adelaide is right," said Alfred judiciously.

"Sassi's right," said Frank.

"Thank you, Frank," said Sassi.

"I'll have one of each," said Robby.

"Actually," Alfred said, still as judiciously, "I believe I've also heard them spoken of as slapjacks."

"You mean flapjacks," said Kelly.

"No, I don't believe I do. I believe I mean slapjacks."

Jigger strolled in then, looking as sullen as usual, but all at once her face lighted up. She sniffed, looked around happily, and said, "Griddlecakes!"

Everybody spoke at once.

(3)

Couples

"This is fun!" Jigger shouted. Ocean sprayed by on both sides of *Nothing Ventured IV* as, with Kelly at the wheel and Jigger the only passenger, it roared out of the cove and into the open sea.

Jigger had started her campaign with Kelly at lunchtime, by offering to make his sandwich. He'd accepted, with some apparent surprise, and she'd said, "I was kind of mean to you yesterday, that's why. I want to make up for it."

He had believed her, of course. Jigger considered her lifework to be getting men to believe she was interested in them, and she'd spent most of her waking hours since the onset of puberty in improving her abilities in that direction. Dealing with a recluse like Kelly was duck soup, and it was simplicity itself, after lunch, to get him to take her for a spin in his boat, which was obviously his pride and joy. If she couldn't come back from this joyride with the boat key in her possession, she might as well turn in her false eyelashes.

It had been both surprising and disheartening when Sassi had refused to join her in planning an escape from these clowns—visions of the eternal friendship that would follow their successful escape together had kept Jigger awake most of the night—but Miss Rushby's approach this morning had been second best and she was willing to settle for it. And the plan was a good one. Jigger was to get her hands on the key to *Nothing Ventured IV,* and tonight, after the kidnappers had gone to sleep, they would escape in the boat, the three women. (Actually, Jigger was still slightly confused about Miss Rushby's status here, since at times she seemed kidnapper and at times victim, but with collaborators in such short supply, she couldn't be choosy. All she could do was use whoever was willing to work with her, and keep her eyes open.)

Now, out of the cove, Jigger watched Kelly throttle the boat back and set the wheel so they'd continue untended in a slow straight line. When he was done, she took his hand and said, "Come on, I'll make us drinks."

"All right," he said.

In a way, it was like taking candy from a baby. Kelly so *wanted* to trust somebody. Jigger felt a little bad about what she was doing, and had to keep reminding herself she was dealing here not with a poor sad shnook but with a vicious kidnapper who had to be outwitted.

Still, he *looked* a lot like a poor sad shnook.

She made drinks—hers weak, his strong—and they sat

side by side on the sofa.

"If you don't mind my saying so, Kelly," Jigger said, "you just don't look like a kidnapper."

"I'm not a kidnapper," Kelly said, with a touch of that bad temper that always lurked near his surface. "You think I do this kind of thing all the time?"

"Why do it at all?" she asked him.

"Why? I've been forced to, that's why!"

How fiery he looked. "Who forced you?" she asked him. She'd started this conversation simply to have something to talk about, but now she was really interested, because she suddenly had the feeling that no one would ever force this guy Kelly into anything.

"Society!" he cried, and angrily flung up the hand that didn't hold the drink.

"Society? What do you mean, society?"

He glared at her with brooding eyes. "I mean that society has made no place for me," he said through clenched teeth. "So I have to carve my own place in this world, no matter who gets in my way."

She blinked. She hadn't expected anything like this from Kelly. All she'd ever seen from him so far was petulant shnookdom. This was the other side of the coin and she was finding it a contradictory but compelling combination: a shnook with fire.

And then what he was saying finally connected with her, and she realized that her own attitude was exactly the same as his. No place had been made for her in the world either, and she was determined to carve her own, and it didn't matter who got in her way.

"I understand, Kelly," she said. "I know just what you mean."

He looked surprised. "You do?"

"Yes, I do," she said fiercely. "You have to fight for what you want in this life."

"That's right! You do know, don't you?" He swigged from his drink, thumped the glass down on a table.

"Of course I know!" she told him. "You don't get anything in this life that you don't fight for."

"That's for sure." He grinned at her in savage companionship. "And you know what the only weapon is?"

She did. "Money!" she cried.

"That's right!" His fists were clenched, his face was flushed. "Money is power!"

"That's right, Kelly, you're right!" She was caught up in it completely now, she was clutching at his arm, she'd never felt so totally understood by another human being in her entire life. She'd forgotten all about her belief that Kelly was a shnook, she'd forgotten all about Miss Rushby and the key, she'd forgotten all about Sassi Manoon and the perfect entree into the movies. There was nothing but Kelly, who understood! He understood! "We've got to get it any way we can!" she yelled, exultant.

"And then they'll leave us alone!" Kelly roared. He was gripping her arms, his hands like steel.

"To live our own lives!" she yelled in his face, laughing at the wonder of it, the beauty of it, this meeting of star-crossed atoms.

"Yes!"

"Yes!"

"JIGGER!"

"KELLY!"

They flung themselves into a wild embrace, and only much later did they begin to be gentle.

Sassi came out of the water, removed her bathing cap, and walked across the white sand to where she'd left the blanket. Lying face down on it, she gave herself up to sunlight and ease.

Ease. How long had it been since she'd felt ease? How long since she'd been calm and comfortable? There was always something, there had been always something for years now. When was the last time she'd awakened and been able to say, "I have nothing at all to do today"? Seven years at least.

The image she'd thought of yesterday still pleased her. This was a business deal, in which she was being kept from work until the studio produced a certain number of dollars. A deal like that was the easiest thing in the world to understand, and, in fact, the only other times in recent years she'd been able to relax at all had been when her advisors were holding out for more money. This was simply a variant on contract talks.

But a lovely variant. This time, there weren't even personal appearances to fill in the gap. No planes to catch, no autographs to sign, no interviews to give, no stills to pose for, no Bennys to bitch at. Lovely.

Her guest room had included a drawerful of bathing suits, two in her size, plus bathing caps. She had the run of the island. The food was simple but plentiful, her time was her own, the ocean was lovely, the sun was magnificent, and at the moment she didn't care if these particular contract negotiations went on for six months.

Someone sat down near her. Suspecting it was The Weasel

again — her private name for Jigger — she kept her eyes shut, pretending to be asleep. The Weasel thought they were in a prison-break movie. She'd come sneaking into Sassi's room in the middle of last night, waking her up with a lot of numskull plans, the plans she'd been thwarted from unveiling in the bar. Like rowing out to sea in one of the dinghys: "We'd be found in a couple hours. There's plenty ships out there." Sure. Or like sneaking around at night and barricading everybody else in their rooms. Or like breaking into the radio room. Or God knows what all. Sassi had tried to explain it to her, telling her, "Honey, they're not being tough on us now. We've got it made. You try some dumb stunt, they'll lock you in a coal bin." But The Weasel was insistent, and finally Sassi had had to go under the covers and put her fingers in her ears until she'd gone away.

So was she back now? Someone was there, just off to the right. Sassi, lying on her stomach, kept her eyes closed and her face hidden in the crook of her arm, because if it was The Weasel she didn't want any more escape plans. No tunnels under the sea to Jamaica, no balloons constructed of bedsheets, no scuffing HELP in the sand. No.

But it wasn't The Weasel after all, because finally it was Lee Marvin's voice that said, "You're about done on that side, lady. Better turn over."

"Hello, Frank," she said, eyes still shut. She rather liked Frank, much in the same way she liked Kama and Sutra. He was an enjoyable pet, even if he did have one or two bad habits.

He did Thomas Mitchell now: "A man can forget everything in these islands. Even himself."

"No more imitations, Frank," she said. She opened her

eyes—everything was tinged in red—and looked at him, sitting there on a blanket of his own beside her. "I'm really not up to it," she said.

He shrugged, and looked embarrassed. "Okay," he said.

"How long do you think we'll be here?" she asked, both to ease his embarrassment and because she really wanted to know.

"Not long," he said. "We're supposed to get the ransom tomorrow. If we do, we'll leave here and send the authorities a message where to pick you up."

"What if you don't?"

Frank looked embarrassed again and shrugged. "I dunno. We'll have to work it out then, I guess."

A trace of cold touched Sassi's spine. "You wouldn't— *do* anything, would you?"

"What?" He looked startled, then laughed in confusion. "Heck, *no*. What do you think we are? I guess we'll just give them another message. Maybe put you on the radio and tell them you're alive and well."

"Sure," Sassi said, much relieved. "Anything to oblige." She found herself hoping it would happen that way: no ransom tomorrow, and then another demand, and so on. With any luck she could get a couple weeks out of this. And it could happen that way. If she knew Joshua Solly, and God knew she did, he wouldn't be in any hurry to cough up a lot of money, not for her or anybody. "How much are you asking?" she wanted to know.

"Four hundred thousand."

"I get twice that much for a picture," she said, feeling idiotically that it was an insult to be held for such little ransom.

"Eight-fifty you get," he said. "We were going to ask that,

but we thought it was too much."

"It wouldn't hurt to try," she said.

He shrugged. "We settled for four."

"Always start high," she advised him. "You can always settle for less later on. I wish you'd told me before."

"I didn't think you'd care," he said.

She laughed and sat up. "This is a nutty conversation," she said. "How'd you get into something like this, anyway?"

Frank grinned. "Which story do you want to hear? The sick old mother that needs the operation, or the kid brother in medical school?"

"Okay," Sassi said. "I deserved that."

Which made Frank embarrassed again. "It was kind of snotty," he said. "Actually, I just want the money."

"What if you get caught?"

"I'd rather not."

"But what if you do?"

Frank grinned again. "I'd rather not," he said.

Sassi saw that was the only answer she was going to get, so she lay down again, on her back this time, and said, "If you do, I probably won't identify you."

He looked at her in surprise. "Why not?"

"Because you're a nice guy," she said, "and prison would probably be bad for your disposition."

Smiling, he said, "Thanks, then. But I hope the question never comes up."

"One thing," she said.

"What's that?"

"Don't spoil it, you know? Don't try to kiss me or make out with me or anything like that. Okay?"

It was Billy DeWolfe who answered: "Oh, my dear, I wouldn't do a thing like *that.*"

DONALD E. WESTLAKE

Sassi laughed and shut her eyes. "Don't let me sleep more than an hour," she said.

"Right," said Frank.

*

Jigger glared at herself in the bathroom mirror. "Jigger Jackson," she said savagely, "you're a goddam fool. In the first place, the guy's a kidnapper, he'll die on the gallows. In the second place, he's a nut, he'll blow himself up some day. And in the third place, Sassi Manoon is the only one around here that can do you any good." She squinted balefully at her image in the mirror. "So why fall for a creep like Kelly?"

Her image didn't answer.

She looked away from herself, disgusted, and glared instead at the key in her open palm. The fact that it was the wrong key made it both less and more than she wanted to do. So now what? Eh? Now what?

She and Kelly had stayed out there on the boat all day, Kelly having cut the engine so they could just drift wherever the gentle waves took them. They hadn't even started for home until long after dark, after the nearly-full moon was already up and gleaming its sweet pale falsehoods on the black ocean. And it wasn't till then, till they were already on their way back to the island, that she thought again of the key. It was in use just then, of course, but might he have an extra?

The thought saddened her. She was troubled about having to do this, but she was also determined. It didn't matter about the moonlight or Kelly's unexpected magnetism or her own feelings, she was out here for a

(*150*)

purpose and she was going to stick to that purpose. Too much was at stake, she couldn't let bright moonlight and stupid emotion spoil things this time. Still, it bothered her.

It bothered her when she went down into the cabin and went through Kelly's pants, he not being in them at the time, and a part of her really didn't want to find a key in there. When her fingers did close on a key, her heart sank.

But then she pulled it out and looked at it, and saw a way out of the dilemma after all, because it was a Yale, and attached to it was a small cardboard tag on which someone had long ago written in ink RADIO ROOM.

Radio room. She tucked the key away inside her own clothing and went back out on deck.

And now here she was, an hour later, alone at last in the third-floor bathroom, looking at herself and at the key and feeling very confused and troubled and irritated and upset.

All right. The compromise she'd worked out was a good one. She and Sassi wouldn't be escaping in the boat, they wouldn't exactly be escaping at all, but the effect would be the same.

It had come to her in a flash, as she'd stood there on the boat with the radio-room key in her hand. What they would do tonight, they would sneak into the radio room and signal for help. Then she would slip a note under Kelly's door, knock on the door until she was sure he was awake, and then she and the other two women would hurry away and hide in the cellars. There were hundreds of places to hide down there; it would take days for anybody to find them. And the note would tell Kelly that help was on its way, that they'd used the radio and the kidnappers should escape at once.

That would do it. Kelly wouldn't be captured, at least not

this time. Sassi Manoon would be rescued, and Jigger would still have the credit. If the plan was sour ashes in her mouth, that just showed how stupid she was, that's all. And if she couldn't help daydreaming about Kelly some night a year or two from now sneaking in her bedroom window to take her in his arms and whisper how he understood, that just showed she'd seen too many movies.

She looked again at her reflection in the mirror. "So let's go," she said, and her reflection nodded, tight-lipped. She left the bathroom and went downstairs to the room Miss Rushby shared with the Major—that was part of the enigma of Miss Rushby—and knocked softly on the door.

Miss Rushby opened almost at once, nodded, touched her finger to her lips, and tiptoed out. "I thought it was you," she whispered, when she had the door closed behind her. "He's asleep. Come along."

They moved silently down the hall and into a sitting room, where Miss Rushby carefully shut the door before switching on the lights. Then she said, "Well? Any success?"

"I got something better than the boat key," Jigger told her. "I got the key to the radio room."

Miss Rushby, an anticipatory smile left hanging on her face like Christmas wreaths in February, said, "Eh? You did what?"

Jigger told her the plan all in a rush, sensing from the outset that Miss Rushby wasn't entirely pleased by the turn of events. But when she was done, Miss Rushby merely nodded in a thoughtful sort of way and said, "May I see the key?"

Jigger handed it over.

Miss Rushby took it, sighed, and said, "Thank you, my dear. You may go to bed now."

"What? What about—?"

"No, dear." Miss Rushby, smiling sadly, shook her head. "There will be no messages. No rescues. No escapes. I'd thought you would prove useful, but a workman is no better than the tools he uses, as they say. Well, well, I'll think of something else. Good night, my dear." And she left the room.

Jigger's mouth hung open five seconds while her mind rearranged the facts at its disposal—Miss R one of the kidnappers, in league with the Major, using her to help double-cross Kelly and the other two—and then it shut with a snap and she stormed purposefully back up to the third floor to let Kelly know what she'd done and what Miss Rushby and the Major had been planning to do.

He wasn't there. She went looking for him, getting more and more frantic, and fifteen minutes later she found him in the library on the second floor, listening to Miss Rushby.

Jigger stopped in front of them. "You gave him back the key," she said.

Miss Rushby smiled her sad smile. "Of course, dear," she said. "Good night, Kelly." She got to her feet and left the room.

Jigger said, "Kelly—"

"Never mind," Kelly said. He was looking at the key in his hand. "A long long time ago," he said, "I learned something. I forgot it for a while today. Now I remember it again." He got to his feet. He wouldn't look at her, she couldn't see into his eyes.

"Please, Kelly," she said. "Let me explain."

He walked out of the room.

Jigger stood there a minute or two longer, but there was nothing to do. She couldn't run after him, she couldn't explain, she couldn't say a word. So she went off to bed instead, where she amazed and infuriated herself by crying herself to sleep.

(4)

Smiles and Frowns

Robby loved mornings like this—the sky a cloudless blue, the air soft and warm, the sea calm and sparkling beneath the sun. There'd been another great communal breakfast this morning—though Jigger and Kelly had both been absent this time—and there'd been a feeling of their all being on vacation somehow, at a camp or a lodge, off with a congenial group for a special time separate from everybody's normal life. And now here he was standing on the deck of *Nothing Ventured IV,* about to sail out across the beautiful blue and yellow day and come back with armloads of beautiful green. Who could ask for anything more?

Kelly came up on deck now, apparently having spent the entire night playing kalah with Starnap, and Robby said, "You ready?"

"Of course I'm ready," snapped Kelly. "Don't I look ready?"

"You don't have to bite my head off," Robby said. "I just asked if you were ready."

"Well, I am." Kelly's mouth was curved down at the corners.

"You're in an awful mood today," Robby said.

"Is it any of your business?"

Robby shook his head. "No. It's just that, for a man about to go out in the ocean and pick up four hundred thousand dollars, you don't act very happy, that's all. All right, I'm going."

He went on down to the main cabin, where the Major was sitting at his ease, a gin and tonic in one hand and a plastic-tipped cigar in the other. "I guess we'll be on our way in a minute," Robby said.

The Major looked at his watch. "Excellent," he said.

Robby went over to the bar and made himself a drink. Through the porthole he could see a bit of the beach, see Frank and Sassi Manoon sitting there on a blanket with bathing suits on. He wondered if Frank was making out with Sassi Manoon. Today would be a good time for him to do it, while he was alone on the island with just the women.

The boat abruptly started, with an unnecessarily severe jerk, making Robby slop tonic water. He said something about Kelly under his breath, wiped it up with a bar rag, and went over to sit down opposite the Major, who seemed absorbed in contemplation of his cigar smoke.

Robby cast about for a minute or two, trying to find a topic of conversation, but finally admitted to himself that there was none, that he and the Major were not destined to sit around together and chat. He knew about people like the Major. They still lived in another age, where all the people around them were white, and if a black skin did show up, it was a uniform for a servant. It confused them to have the servant sit down like anybody else. Robby thought sometimes he should feel compassion for people like that, locked into unreality, but he couldn't quite get that objective. What he felt was irritation. They bugged him.

Speaking of which, he wondered what was the matter with Kelly. Something sure had him in a hell of a mood.

Well. With Kelly carrying on up on deck and the Major being rigidly polite down here, it was going to be a great trip. Wonderful trip.

Robby put his nose in his drink.

*

Sassi rolled over, stretched, opened her eyes, and said, "You know what?"

Frank, sitting beside her with a cigarette dangling in his mouth, looked away from his study of the blue horizon and said, "No, what?"

"I hope you don't get it."

Frank took the cigarette from his mouth. "You hope I don't get what?"

"The money."

He grinned. "Sure."

"No, I mean it." She sat up. "Can I have a cigarette?"

"Sure." He lit one from his and gave it to her. "You want to call our bluff, huh?"

"Heck, no," she said. "I'm just enjoying it here, that's all."

Frank smiled experimentally. "Of course you are," he said.

"Brother," she said, "you should have my life for a week. It's like an iceberg: the ten percent you see is all white and sparkly, but the other ninety percent is cold and wet and dark and no fun at all. Sassi Manoon is mostly done with mirrors."

"I would've brought my violin," Frank said, "but salt water plays hell with the wood."

She grinned at him and shook her head. "You bastard, you won't ever let me have my big scene. How can I feel sorry for myself with you around?"

"How can you help but?"

"You're not so bad," she said "In fact, you're pretty good."

"Yeah," he said, "but don't spoil it, you know? No kissing me or making out or anything like that."

She laughed aloud. She didn't know when she'd been happier. "Frank," she said, "I hope they *never* pay. I hope you have to keep me here forever!"

*

Quietly, "sprong" said the radio-room door.

Jigger, screwdriver held in both hands, looked up and down the hall. Nobody. Sassi Manoon and her boy friend were out on the beach together, and the Rushby fink was napping in her room down on the second floor. Jigger took a deep breath and stepped into the room.

The door wouldn't close completely any more, but it was good enough. If she had bad luck and somebody came up to the third floor, they'd hear her anyway, whether the door was closed or not.

She switched on the light and looked at the bank of electronic equipment hulking enigmatically along the opposite wall, staring at her blank-faced with all its dials. "Damn it," she whispered.

The window was to the right, and faced the sea. She went over and saw Sassi and Frank lying on the blanket, but could no longer see *Nothing Ventured IV.* It was out there somewhere in all that ocean.

She was *not* going to cry. She was going to turn on that radio and contact the police, being sure to leave enough time so she could warn Kelly and the others and give them a chance to get away. She had to do at least that much, no matter what.

She thought about movie contracts, the publicity she would get out of this, the chances for stardom, and she tried to ignore how flat and uninteresting it all sounded. It was what she'd wanted all her life, and now it was within her grasp and how *stupid* to let an emotional hang-up spoil it now. Kelly was lost to her anyway, she might as well get *something* she wanted out of all this, whether she wanted it or not.

She turned away from the window and sat down in the swivel chair in front of the microphone. There was a switch near her right hand that said On-Off, and it was turned to Off, and she turned it instead to On. Then she cleared her throat, leaned close to the mike, and said, "Hello? Hello?"

*

The two submarine sleds came slicing through the water like flat sharks. Kelly rode one and Robby the other, their feet against the padded boards at the rear of the sleds, their hands on the handlebars. They wore bathing suits, air tanks, rubber gloves, utility belts, and goggles.

They had stopped *Nothing Ventured IV* a good distance from the drop zone, and from its deck they'd watched the two helicopters appear far to the east, the one veering westward and gradually fading from sight, the other hovering in one place for a moment or two, then circling around and heading south again, its mission obviously done.

The Major had pointed, saying, "That other chap's the lookout. Up where you can't see him for the sun."

"Just like we figured," Robby'd said.

"We'll be back soon," Kelly had said then, still surly. He'd spent most of the trip out from the island down with Starnap, playing kalah.

They'd dropped the sleds over the side, jumped over after them, started them, and headed north, keeping eight to ten feet below the surface, skimming along through a dark green-blue world in which an occasional fish looked at them pop-eyed as they passed, then itself darted away into the even darker depths below.

They were both good at the sleds now, having practiced with them around Montego Bay every chance they'd gotten in the last week. It had originally been Frank and Robby who were supposed to operate the sleds, but Frank turned out to have something weird wrong with his sense of balance or something. Whatever it was, it made him invariably steer the sled on a downward slant, and he had to be pulled to the surface every time. In shallow water this merely meant he stirred up mud when he hit bottom, but out in the deep ocean it would be goodbye, Frank. So Kelly had taken over.

They had an hour of air in the two tanks on their backs. The drop was nearly six miles from where they'd left the boat, and it took the best part of half an hour to get there. But when they did arrive, it was a snap. Nothing to it. Kelly held both sleds while Robby used his knife to cut through the straps holding the package and the marker buoy together. They tied the package to Robby's sled, and then turned and headed back again, two flat shadow creatures flying through a blue-green world with an orange roof.

And now, ahead, there was the flashlight suspended in the water below *Nothing Ventured IV* turning this way and that with the movement of the water, guiding them home.

They surfaced beside the boat, the Major threw a line over to them, and they climbed aboard, Robby going first, towing his sled up after him.

When Kelly and the other sled were aboard, they untied the dripping package and carried it down into the main cabin, where the Major carefully cut it open.

Green.

They stood looking at it in awed respect, and gradually all three of them began to smile. Even Kelly seemed to have forgotten his bad mood for the moment.

The Major broke the silence. "Gentlemen," he said, "fortune has smiled upon us."

"And now," Robby said, "we smile upon our fortune."

"Let's get back," said Kelly.

(5)

Dos Equis

Miss Rushby checked the Webley, found it in proper working order, fully loaded and safely on safety. She then checked her slip, found it wasn't showing, and left the bedroom.

She'd hoped all three of them would be on the beach, but the Jigger girl was missing. Too bad, but not vital. Frank was the important one to worry about.

Actually, she was sorry about what she'd had to do to Jigger, and she was just as pleased not to have to meet the girl's eyes directly just now, when she would be having so much else to concentrate on.

Her sensible shoes really weren't very sensible when it came to walking on sand, and she traveled across it in long slow strides as though in imitation of someone walking through waist-deep water. She stopped where Frank and Sassi were sitting together on a blanket, and said, "Good afternoon."

Frank looked around. "Hi, Miss R."

"Hello, Frank." Miss Rushby showed him the Webley. "Hands up," she said.

*

"Gently," said the Major. "We don't want to drop that in the ocean."

"We know," said Robby, with only a trace of apparent sarcasm. He was in the process of handing the bulky package of money over the side to Kelly, who was standing in the dinghy. The Major, also in the dinghy, was holding it steady against the side of *Nothing Ventured IV.*

Kelly got the package and lowered it gently into the dinghy, then helped his friend over the side and in. "I'll row," Robby said. No one contradicted him, so he rowed. Kelly sat in the prow, twisted around to face the shore, and the Major sat in the stern, smiling benignly on his two partners.

Adelaide was waiting on shore, the signal that everything was all right. The Major had a strong sudden impulse to smile broadly and wave his arms at her, but that would be undignified and childish, so he contented himself with a small smile and a small nod of the head, neither of which she could see.

The dinghy pulsed toward shore, Robby rowing with practiced ease. The shore itself was in shadow now, the sun low enough to be hidden behind the bulk of the house and the island, but out here on the water it still peeked over the manor roof, glaring suspiciously into the Major's eyes and making him squint.

Robby timed it nicely, giving one last strong heave on the oars just in conjunction with a long rolling wave that carried them well inshore and receded with the first third of the boat beached on nearly dry sand.

"We're here," said Kelly, with satisfaction, and Robby shipped the oars.

The Major withdrew his Walther automatic and pointed it at Robby. "On your feet, gentlemen," he said. He could see Adelaide, onshore, pointing her Webley at Kelly.

Kelly, outraged, cried, "What's the meaning of this?"

"The meaning," the Major told him, with a smile of crocodile sadness, "is that our partnership is most regrettably at an end."

*

Jigger didn't believe it at first, when she saw the guns come out. She was watching from the third-floor window of the radio room, and her plan had been to make another attempt to talk to Kelly as soon as he was away from the others, but now she didn't know what to do. She watched the Major and Miss Rushby march Kelly and Robby away at gunpoint —come to think of it, Frank and Sassi didn't seem to be around any more either—and for just a minute everything seemed hopelessly lost.

But then she saw the package in the dinghy. The Major had left it there, obviously intending to come right back with Miss Rushby after Kelly and Robby had been locked away, when he and Miss Rushby would get into the dinghy, row out to their own boat, and be long gone with the boodle when the fuzz got here.

Oh, yeah?

Jigger got moving.

There were stairs and there were stairs, and it seemed to Jigger she could count on characters like the Major and Miss Rushby being too snooty to use the servants' stairs at the back of the house. And she was right. She flew down the back stairs like the slender ghost of a wronged scullery maid, hit the beach running, made a U-turn at the dinghy with only enough slackening of pace to grab the plastic-covered package up in both arms, and tore back into the house at a dead run.

She slid to a stop in the deserted main entrance hall. The primary staircase led up from here, and most of the house connected to this hall one way or another. Jigger put her head back and bellowed, *"I called the cops from the radio room!"* She had good projection, she'd worked on that during her one season as an apprentice in a summer stock theater in Pennsylvania. Wherever they were in the house, the Major and Miss Rushby had heard her.

Jigger listened to the echoes die away, nodded in satisfaction, and took off for the cellars.

*

The Major had just locked the door behind Robby and Kelly—he'd put them next door to the other two—when he heard the shout. He stopped where he was, listening, heard nothing more, and turned to Adelaide. "That girl?"

(*165*)

Adelaide was wide-eyed, as so he supposed was he. "Could she have?" she asked.

"We must find out," said the Major.

He was faster than Adelaide, of course, and she hadn't finished climbing the stairs to the third floor when he was already at the broken door of the radio room, looking in and seeing the rig still on and lit. "Turn around, my dear," he called. "It's all true."

He caught up with her as she made the turn at the second floor. They were both a bit out of breath, but they kept going. "Do you think," Adelaide said, hurrying as best she could, "we can make it?"

"We can only try, my dear." The Major held her elbow on the descent, not to hurry but to help.

"At least," she said, as they reached the first floor at last and headed for the door, "we have the money."

"Thank heaven," said the Major.

Then they got to the dinghy, and they didn't have the money after all. "And to think," Adelaide said angrily, "I was actually feeling sorry for that girl!"

"A nasty little baggage," the Major said. "I never liked her, never."

Adelaide wrung her hands. "What shall we do?"

The Major turned to glare at the house. Faces looked back from second-story windows, but none of them was Jigger. Twenty-seven rooms. Three basements. Plus an entire jungle out back.

"We'll never find her," the Major said. "Not in time."

"We'll have to go without?"

"I'm afraid so, my dear."

He helped her into the dinghy, pushed it into the water,

wetting his shoes and trouser legs, then climbed in himself and began to row.

"Poor Percy," said Adelaide.

(6)

Love

Kelly stood at the window watching *Redoubtable* sail out of the tiny cove and away. Evening was lengthening toward night, the beach looked deserted, *Nothing Ventured IV* looked abandoned as it bobbed down there in the water, the future looked grim. The Major and Miss Rushby had gotten away with the money, Jigger had called the police, and the whole plan had gone up the flue.

Kelly heard somebody kick the door open behind him, but he didn't turn around till he heard Frank call his name: "Kelly? Time for us to get out of here, buddy."

Kelly nodded, turned away from the disappearing *Redoubtable,* and walked wearily across the room. "I know."

Robby said, "Next time," but then let it go at that.

Kelly just shrugged. Later on, he knew, he'd go talk

things over with Starnap and maybe they'd think of something else to do, but at the moment it all seemed hopeless. They'd exposed their faces and their real names, they'd used up their cash reserve, and now they had nothing to show for it and no way to organize themselves to start all over again.

Sassi came to the doorway, looking in at them, seeming almost as troubled as they were, saying, "You boys better get going."

Robby said, "I hate it that the Major got the money."

Frank said, "He didn't. We watched Jigger go out and grab it while you guys were being marched up here."

Kelly lifted his head, feeling sudden hope. "They didn't get the money? It's still on the island?"

"Forget it," Frank told him. "You'd never find it before the cops got here."

"But—Jigger—"

Frank shook his head in disgust. "Not Jigger," he said. "She wasn't saving that dough for us. Don't you know what she's up to?"

It was a question Kelly had already been gnawing on for quite a while without finding any satisfactory answer. "No," he said.

"A movie contract," Frank told him. "She figures to parlay this caper into an in at the studio. Isn't that right, Sassi?"

"It'll work, too," Sassi said. "The publicity alone would help a lot, but besides that, she's saved the studio's money. And if I put in a word for her too—" She shrugged.

Frank said, "You? Why?"

"She'll make a deal with me," Sassi said. "We'll both get your descriptions wrong."

"It almost isn't worth it," Frank said.

"It's worth it to me," said Robby. "What about you, Kelly?"

Kelly shook his head. "I don't know," he said. "Let's just get out of here."

"Right."

They left the room and started for the stairs and Jigger popped into sight at the end of the hall. Coming briskly toward them, she said, "Kelly, I want to talk to you."

"Hello, sweetheart," said Frank.

Jigger stopped in front of them, looking at Kelly. "Kelly? Will you listen to me?"

Kelly didn't want to. All he wanted was to get back on his ship and go away from here somewhere and let this day come to an end and maybe play some kalah with Starnap and then tomorrow possibly start thinking again. He said, wearily, "We don't have the time," and kept walking toward the stairs.

Jigger folded her arms and stepped to one side, letting him by. "If that's the way you want it," she said.

They all walked by her, but Kelly got only as far as the head of the stairs. He stopped there and looked back at Jigger, the others all stopping, too, and looking at him in confusion. Jigger was still standing there, arms folded, a tough expression on her face. What did she want to talk to him about? He said, "Where's the money?"

"Will you listen to me?"

What was this going to be? Some sort of self-justification. He shrugged and said, "Go ahead and talk."

"In private," she said, and nodded her head at the nearest doorway. "In there."

Frank said, "Kelly, we don't have much time."

Kelly had no idea why he wanted to hear what Jigger had to say—what could she have to say?—but for some reason it seemed important to listen. He said to the others, "Go on down, I'll be a minute."

Frank said, "Kelly—"

"Come on Frank," Robby said. To Kelly he said, "Try not to take too long."

"I won't."

Frank and Robby and Sassi went downstairs, and Kelly followed Jigger into the room. As soon as they were inside he said, "Where's the money?"

"In the cellar," she said. "Down the first flight of stairs, behind the third door on the left."

"Fine," said Kelly, and left the room. He went to the head of the stairs and called, *"Frank!"*

"What?"

"Look in the cellar, first flight of stairs, third door on the left."

"Right."

He looked back at the doorway and Jigger was standing there. He said, "I guess I don't have to listen to anything else, do I?"

"You don't have to," Jigger said.

"Right," said Kelly, and started down the stairs. He went half a flight, expecting her to call him back, and when she didn't, he turned around and went back up and said, "Why'd you tell me where it was?"

"Because you asked me."

Kelly thumped his fist on the banister. "Why did you have to take that key?"

(171)

"Because I was a klutz. I figured to call the cops and then warn you so you could get away before they got here. So I could have my cake and eat it, too."

"What's that supposed to mean?"

"It's supposed to mean I wanted a movie contract and I wanted you, and I was trying to figure out how to get both."

"You wanted me," Kelly said sarcastically, trying to convince himself she was lying and he didn't care.

"Yes," she said. "I still do. That's why I didn't call the cops after all."

From downstairs Frank's voice roared, *"Got it!"*

Kelly blinked, looking in two directions at once. "What? You didn't call?"

"Hear me, Kelly?"

"I hear you, I hear you!"

"I didn't call," Jigger said. "When I got down to it, actually sitting there in that radio room, I had to make up my mind which I wanted more. You, or the movies." She shrugged. "So I made my choice."

"Kelly, let's go!"

Kelly looked down the stairs, then back at Jigger. "You saved our bacon," he said.

"Sure," she said.

He hesitated, looking at her, afraid to take the plunge.

Feet pounded up the stairs, and Robby panted into view. Staring up at them, he gasped, "Kelly! They're here! The cops are here!"

(7)

Virtue Triumphant

Kelly stared at Jigger, and her face drained of color. "I didn't," she said. "Kelly, I didn't. I swear, I swear I didn't."

He kept staring at her, and then slowly he nodded. "All right," he said.

She began to smile. "Thank you, Kelly."

Robby said, "Kelly?"

"Coming."

They all raced downstairs. Frank was standing by a window there, pointing his thumb upward. "In the sky," he said. "In the sky."

Kelly stuck his head out the window and there it was, a lone helicopter high in the sky, hovering like an insect from another planet. He pulled his head back in and said, "We've got to do something."

Robby said, "We can't outrun a helicopter."

"I know, I know."

Sassi said, "He isn't landing, he's just staying up there."

"Waiting for reinforcements," Kelly said. "They must have a lot of planes out, searching this whole area." He shook his head. "I have to talk to Starnap," he said, and before anyone else could say anything, he ran out of the house and down the beach toward the dinghy.

He felt very slow and very visible. He didn't look up, but he could feel the helicopter on the top of his head, like a magnifying glass focusing the sun's rays.

He sculled the dinghy briskly through the calm water to *Nothing Ventured IV*, clambered aboard, and hurried down the steps and into the forward cabin, where he switched on the light and Starnap's control panel.

It took him two minutes to feed the problem into Starnap and less than one minute to get the answer. He read it, frowned, asked another question, looked at the answer, smiled, got to his feet, shut everything off, and raced back up the stairs, over the side, and into the dinghy. He rowed like mad for shore and dashed across the sand and into the house. He burst in, breathless from exertion, and just stood there a few seconds gasping while the others all milled around him asking him what did Starnap say, what were they supposed to do, was there any hope at all.

Kelly took a deep breath. "Starnap," he panted, "Starnap —says—call—the police!"

*

(*174*)

"Well," the policeman with the mustache said to Kelly, "how does it feel to be a hero?"

"We didn't do anything," Kelly said modestly. "The kidnappers were already gone when we got here. They got the money and left."

They were all sitting in the main living room, Kelly and Jigger on one sofa, Frank and Robby and Sassi on another, three policemen in plainclothes on a third. The manor was full of policemen, uniformed and non, American and Jamaican and British. The sky and the beach were full of helicopters, the cove was full of boats. The booty was stashed aboard *Nothing Ventured IV,* and they were all heroes.

The policeman with the mustache took time out to light a pipe, then said, "As I understand it, you four were just out on a pleasure cruise, is that it? You, these two gentlemen, and this young lady."

"My fiancée," Kelly said, taking Jigger's hand.

"Congratulations. And you stumbled across this island, is that how it happened?"

"The place looked interesting," Kelly said. "We didn't think there was anybody here at all until we came into the cove and Miss Manoon waved to us."

The policeman smiled around his pipe and turned to Sassi. "That must have been quite a moment for you, I expect, Miss Manoon," he said.

"It certainly was," Sassi said. "Up till then, I didn't even know if I was going to be alive now."

"This heavy-set man with the German accent," the policeman said, "the one you say seemed to be the ringleader. He threatened your life?"

"He kept—insinuating," Sassi said. She shivered. "I never knew what he was going to do. Any of them."

"But you heard none of them referred to as Baby Face Preble?"

Sassi frowned. "Baby Face Preble? No. I couldn't imagine any of them being called Baby Face anything."

"Mm." The policeman pulled on his pipe, then said, as though reluctantly, "You didn't see anything of a rug, did you? A Persian carpet."

"A rug? Where?"

One of the other policemen said, "It's an entirely different case, Miss Manoon, don't worry your head about it." He turned to the first policeman and said, "I *told* you it was a different case."

"Then why was the truck stolen?" demanded the first policeman. "What happened to the rug? What about the man in the projection booth, described as looking very much like Baby Face Preble?"

"A different case," the other policeman insisted. "An entirely different case, as I've maintained all along." He turned to Sassi, saying, "There's been some controversy over a different set of criminals active the same day you were kidnapped. There are those, like my friend here, who insisted the two gangs were both involved in the same affair."

"Then what *were* the carpet thieves after?" demanded the first policeman.

The second policeman looked condescendingly at him. "A carpet, I should think."

The first policeman puffed out a lot of pipe smoke.

Kelly said, "It's getting late, it's after ten o'clock. I have to get my fiancée home."

The second policeman said, "There'll be reporters on their way, you know. Photographers. Wouldn't you like to stay and talk to them?"

"No," said Kelly. He floundered for a second, then said, "My parents, uh, they don't know anything about my, uh, my fiancée."

"Ah," said the policeman.

"I'd rather they didn't know," Kelly said. "Until the marriage."

"Of course," said the policeman. "You'd like us to downplay your part in the affair."

Kelly nodded. "Yes," he said.

"I think that could be arranged," the policeman said. He looked at the other two. "Don't you think so?"

Adjusting their ties, smoothing their hair, they both said they thought so.

Kelly got to his feet, holding Jigger's hand, and she stood beside him. "Well," he said. "I guess we'll be off, then. Goodbye, Miss Manoon. It was certainly a pleasure to meet you."

Sassi smiled, no more than the situation warranted, and said, "You were life-savers, you and your friends."

Frank and Robby were on their feet now, looking modest and pleased. Frank said, "Shucks, ma'am, we didn't do anything."

"I won't forget what you've all done for me," Sassi said.

Everybody shook hands all around, and then Kelly and Jigger and Frank and Robby left, walking by helicopter light down to the dinghy, rowing out to *Nothing Ventured IV,* driving the ship slowly out of the cove and out to sea.

Sassi Manoon stood at the front window, watching the

lights of the small ship disappear. One of the policemen stood beside her, and after a moment he said, "You know, Miss Manoon, it's young people like that give me hope for the future."

"Me, too," said Sassi Manoon.

About the Author

DONALD E. WESTLAKE is one of our best-known humorous fiction writers, with a busy career already behind him: a term with the Air Force in Germany, editorial work for a literary agency, a season as an actor in stock, a prolific quantity of mystery and science-fiction stories in most of the better magazines, a suspense novel (or two) a year regularly since 1960 — plus three motion pictures already released and a number of others now filming. He was born in Brooklyn, grew up in Albany, New York, and at present lives in New Jersey.